MW01228535

TO BE CLAIMED

BOOK TWO

WILLOW WINTERS

WALL STREET JOURNAL & USA TODAY BESTSELLING AUTHOR

From USA Today best-selling author, Willow Winters, comes a tempting tale of fated love, lust-filled secrets and the beginnings of an epic war.

There was never a question of whether or not I would be his. It's simply what fate demanded.

There's a knowing when the werewolves find their mates. It's an aching need, a desperation... one they would die for. But for their mates, it's a trance, a pull, a submissive desire that's at odds with the shadows of my past and how I've learned to survive.

I didn't know how hard I'd fall.
I didn't know what destiny would bring.
I didn't know it then that I would die for him
as he would me.

GENTLE
SCARS

PART I
LOST PUPPY

PROLOGUE

VERONICA

No one is meant to live forever. Even immortals. As a vampire, I knew one day my life would be over. I imagined it would be due to violence.

Not because I fell in love.

"Promise me you won't take the drug anymore." Vince's voice is tight, his plea desperate. The bloodied tears that stain my cheeks fail to stop.

I chose this. I did it for him. For us. If there's a chance for us to have a real life together, one where I won't grow old … One where I could possibly have a child … it's for love. I never asked for a mate. In all my decades, I never felt this deep need.

Just as I never asked to be immortal, and now ...

"Promise me, Veronica." All I can do is slowly nod my head.

I've turned into a fool for him. Become weak for him. I would do anything for him.

"I promise." I whisper the words I know are a lie. No one is meant to live forever and this had to be done.

"I will give you everything you need. I promise you, my love. It could kill you." I sniffle and kiss the crook of his neck. His gentle embrace brings a warmth to my chilled blood. "I would die without you."

He says that, but expects me to live when he's gone from this world. He'll understand. He must. He's my mate and he'll forgive me.

"I love you, Veronica."

"I will love you forever, Vince."

Our forever.

CHAPTER 1

VINCE

WEEKS BEFORE
THE FIRST MOMENT I FELT MY MATE

How the hell did Devin do it? How could he leave his mate after feeling *this*?

My fingers ball into fists as I stand on the stage, stiff and all but snarling.

A burning shock lingers in my blood, chilling my skin with a cold sweat and willing my limbs to go to her. *To my mate.* My heart races, adrenaline coursing through me as the pull to go to her is overwhelming. By order of my Alpha, I'm ignoring the instinctual demand, just as he did last year. With every second my feet stay planted on this damn stage, the pit in my stomach grows larger, twisting and churning. My dry throat closes, threatening to suffocate me. The aching need devours me. I'm practically fucking weak and useless.

I *need* her.

How the hell did he ever wait for the offering? How could he resist when she was so close and he felt *this*?

"You will wait." Devin's command rings loud in my mind. My wolf whines, but settles. *"It hurts."* My teeth grit as another wave of stinging heat rolls over my body, punishing me for disregarding her. My neck arches, straining against all reason. With my muscles coiled, I fight my instincts. I have no intention of going against my Alpha, but this is fucking torture.

"I'm trying."

Our telepathic conversation pauses as the young women hesitantly walk across the stage. They reek of fear and anxiety, and the awful stench is a slap in the face. The reverberation of their shoes clicking against the metal stage continues to get faster and faster as more of them scuttle past us. The Authority demands the humans be deathly afraid of the paranormal species. Given my urge to howl in utter agony at this moment, I imagine I could reduce them all to nightmares and lasting trauma if I openly struggled to control myself.

Containing this visceral reaction is brutal. The fear it creates will be rewarded by the Authority, so perhaps there's a silver lining. The humans' fear is good for us; not so good for the Alpha's mate, though. I can smell her dread from here.

They call her Grace. Although I can barely focus on her, I'm proud to welcome her into our pack. If she knew more about why these treaties exist and what it means to be chosen, I'm sure she wouldn't be so damn terrified. But then again, neither would any of the other humans.

A smirk pulls my lips up; I can faintly hear Dom and Caleb's mate telling Grace something about us having sticks up our asses. The humor relieves the agony for a moment.

"She must've met Dom." I stifle my chuckle at Lev's comment. Grace's friend, Liz, isn't as scared as she should be. Either that or she's putting on a front. I barely resist the urge to turn my head toward Dom to gauge his reaction.

Caleb snickers and says, *"Our mate's a little firecracker, isn't she?"* I can practically feel his grin. Ever since the two of them felt their pull to her, Caleb's excitement has been radiating through all of us and his wolf won't stop panting for her. If he were in wolf form, he'd be drooling with his tongue hanging out of his jaws. Dom's enthusiasm is dampened by his reluctance to share his mate. I'm sure as hell not jealous of those fuckers. Especially not now that I've found my own mate.

Goosebumps spread along my skin. *My mate.*

"Which one is she?" Jude's excited so many of us are finding our mates. Perhaps all of our mates are human. It would be a rarity, but then again, so is the continued existence of our pack.

I search the crowd in the direction of the intense pull I've been denying. My eyes lock on my mate and travel down her body, appreciating every inch. She's wearing a black, pleated leather skirt that ends mid-thigh, making her long legs appear even longer, along with her sheer thigh highs. Her high heels add even more to her height. Still, she's got to be a few inches shorter than me. My gaze longs to strip away each button on her sheer white blouse. Her tanned skin and long black hair, along with her large dark eyes, inform me she's new to the area. We come to this town for the offering every year and I've never seen her or anyone like her; she must've moved here recently. A few strands of iridescent black pearls are settled over her cleavage. Filipino, maybe? I've yet to hear her speak. She drips of sex appeal ... the only thing I'm certain of is that she's mine.

"Mine," my wolf echoes with a growl.

It's evident she was made for me. Her black hair is pulled into a simple bun, exposing her slender neck that's tempting me to bite her. To sink my fangs into the tender flesh and claim her. I stifle my groan as my dick twitches. My hands flex once again before fisting, my blunt nails digging into my skin.

My mate's dark brown eyes are focused on the far right of the stage, then they wander, studying every inch of the stadium and failing to follow my direction. A low growl forms in my chest, scaring the fuck out of the poor girl in front of me.

Shit. I didn't mean that. I'm too damn desperate for her

attention. The need for her to see me nearly overrides my logical side. I need her to watch me like I'm watching her. Just the thought of her locking her eyes on mine makes my cock harden. I can't wait for this damn offering to be over.

My eyes narrow as I continue to stare at her gorgeous body. There's no way she's younger than nineteen. It's not that she looks older; it's something about her poise and the confidence she exudes. She's a woman in every way. My mate should be up here. She should be in line, waiting to offer herself to me so I can take her. Even if she's only just moved here, the terms of the treaty are clear. My heart speeds up with angst pumping through my veins.

What if she'll never be offered because she's older than twenty-one? What if she doesn't live in Shadow Falls at all and she's only visiting? The thought of never seeing my mate again sends a pulse of panicked heat through my body with a force that almost brings me to my knees.

"Calm down, Vince." Devin's stern voice grounds me and I place my hands behind my back.

"I cannot. I cannot lose her, Alpha." Even in my mind, his title is emphasized, both pleading with him and warning.

There's a second of hesitation. Only one, that's tense and severe, before he answers.

"You may stay behind only to find out why she wasn't offered."

"Yes, Alpha." My heartbeat slowly stops hammering in my chest as I continue to watch my mate. As soon as Grace and

Liz are collected and safe in the cars, I'm hunting down those sexy, long legs. *"Thank you."*

"Shut the fuck up; our mates are here." Dom's threateningly low voice makes my lips kick up into a smirk.

"If I didn't know any better, I'd think you were pissed." I can practically feel his rumbling growl.

"Knock it off. Dom, you handle your mate; I'll handle mine. Grace is last, so we won't have to wait. Any questions?"

"No, Alpha." We answer Devin in unison. This should be easy enough. Then I can track down my mate. I've never been so eager for an event to be over in my entire existence. My skin heats with anticipation as Grace walks past me. I can hear her breath steadying as she walks toward Devin. The presence of her mate is already soothing her nerves. *Good.* This will be over soon and then I can stalk my sexy little vixen.

As I walk down the steps, knowing their mates are in place, chaos ensues on stage. It happens far too fast and unexpectedly. With rigid discipline, I don't hesitate; I react. Moving to my position as ordered, I'm calm on the outside, but inwardly there's an equal amount of chaos as there is on stage. Dom's mate is screaming. Her cries are hysterical and they elicit a knee-jerk, involuntary reaction from the onlookers. Her fists pound with violent thuds against his hard body and it feels like a damn bullet to my chest. She's fighting him. She's resisting her mate. It's shocking; it's soul crushing. It takes everything in me to keep my expression neutral and not react.

I can't even imagine how he must feel.

It's not supposed to be like this. I've seen offerings before in my old pack. The women are meant to be calm and go willingly. The bond, even if they don't know a damn thing about it, is strong. It's unbreakable. It's captivating. The touch of a mate is comforting. The only times there are problems at the offerings is when some asshole wolves take what doesn't belong to them. That doesn't happen much now that the Authority has taken over inter- and intraspecies relations.

She doesn't stop. Their mate fights for her life against them.

"Are you sure she's your mate?" Several growls vibrate through me in response. *"I didn't mean that. Shit, I apologize."*

Caleb's voice reaches me through the deafening snarl still coming from Dom. *"Don't worry about it. She'll be all right. She'll be fine."* Even though his words are laced with positivity and confidence, I can feel his apprehension. Those poor fuckers, Dom and Caleb. Their pain permeates through us. The cries of outrage pick up now that the crowd is no longer shocked and other emotions are surfacing. *Double fuck.* If we don't act fast, things are going to get messy.

I'm vaguely aware of Devin's aura pushing down on my shoulders, steadying me. Holding all of us in place and settling our nerves. I'm grateful for it.

Devin's mate fights against his hold as she screams her friend's name, the trance broken. She pushes off of him in a futile attempt to free herself, but in her struggle against him, she's radiating dominance. I flinch at the Alpha waves overwhelming me and look to Devin. He's calmer than still waters, not even affected by her innate influence. I know he felt it, though. We all felt it.

Our Alpha mate.

"Calm her down." Devin finally gives the command to Grace, the words spoken low, gently and she immediately composes herself as if they were a balm she needed. A soothing wind pacifies my nerves, even though Dom's mate is still battering her fists against him. The effect of our Alpha mate's emotions is overwhelming. It's clear she was made for Devin. Together, the two of them exude power. I've been told that an Alpha finding his mate makes him stronger and his pack closer, but to feel it, to be a part of such a strong union—it's all-consuming.

As Grace holds Liz, Dom's sadness and anger creep in. But typical of the beast he is, on the surface he's furious. Grace's powerful force is weakened when she sees his scowl. She's terrified, gripping Liz tighter, protecting her small pack of two.

The air is bitter with their fear.

Devin's hands settle on Grace's shoulders; it does little to assuage the anxiousness rolling off her in waves. It's so strong it's practically choking me. But in an instant, the surges cease and my breath returns. I turn just in time to see Devin catch his mate as she faints. The crowd erupts in outrage and screams of terror. The Authority requires the humans' submission and for us to reinforce it. This is not how I envisioned the day's events. Every second is more somber than the last. My brow furrows in anger, but Devin continues to hold us in place. A fierce growl bursts forth from his throat, carrying through the stadium and silencing the humans.

"Move." He snarls his command and we all walk forward in unison. Devin cradles his unconscious mate in his arms while Liz cries helplessly, weaker by the second, flailing her fists against Dom's back as he carries her over his shoulder like a caveman. The tension pours from him. I can't help but to wonder what's wrong with her. Something is very wrong. Dom's grief ricochets through me as he releases a shaky breath; it's the only indication he's anything other than furious.

"She'll be better once we're back." Caleb's words almost sound like a hopeful question. His panting wolf is whining in agony. I feel nothing but pity for all three of them.

As I lead our pack to the parked cars, my gaze roams the stadium for my mate. But she's gone. The hammering in my chest speeds up as I frantically search for her.

Before panic takes over, I'm given my leave.

"Go, Vince. Do not approach her. You have two hours."

Two hours.

I don't waste a second once Devin grants me permission. My limbs push forward with determination and my wolf claws at my chest to get to her. *I must find my mate.*

CHAPTER 2

VERONICA

A MOMENT BEFORE THE CHAOS
THAT IS THE OFFERING AT SHADOW FALLS

My lips purse in annoyance listening to these foolish mutts snickering as they formulate a shit plan of retribution. I've never felt such a snarl of distaste overwhelm me. My eyes narrow and I bet these wolfish pricks waiting behind the stadium can't even spell the word they chant in unison: *retribution*.

Bitter cold envelops me at feeling the depths of my desire to rip them apart. It's sudden and not welcome. Lifting my chin, I shut out their conversation. It takes more effort than it should, though.

With an uneasy exhale, I return my attention to the stage. My intention was to discuss a proposition with the Alpha on behalf of the coven, but that's not going to happen.

I didn't anticipate his pack finding mates. From what I've heard of Shadow Falls, it hasn't happened in quite a while. So color me surprised by the change of plans. My nails tap impatiently on the metal seat in front of me as I watch both girls struggle against the massive beasts. Fear permeates the air around me and it reminds me of my youth.

For some reason I have a soft spot for the petite blond wolf. Lizzie, if I heard her friend right. I don't know how they can't hear her wolf whining. Someone needs to let it out of its cage. My nose scrunches and my tongue clucks. If they'd calm the hell down, I may still have a chance to speak with Devin. That's all right, though. I'm sure I'll be meeting him soon when my big bad wolf comes to fetch me.

My smirk is at odds with the screams around me, with the humans who cower in terror in their seats. Yet all I can focus on is the beast of a man who dares to stare me down as if I'm his. As if it's his right to take me.

He's so obvious. A small smile plays at my lips while my heart beats with lust. He's fucking adorable. Well, maybe adorable isn't the right word. *Sexy as fuck.* Yes, that's a better description. I could feel his eyes on me ever since he got here, willing me to stare back at him. My smile morphs into a wicked grin. He's going to have to learn that it's not so easy to earn my submission. Hell, I'm used to being the one giving the orders.

"Let's run them off the road," one wolf murmurs beneath his breath just outside the stadium, grabbing my attention once again. Three are certainly werewolves, and one must be something else. Otherwise they wouldn't have needed to speak aloud. Irritation runs through me.

This time I'm even more displeased; they've interrupted the little fantasy I was concocting of my strong, handsome wolf on his knees for me with his tongue between my thighs. Holy hell, I can't wait to enjoy him, play with him. I may even allow him to toy with me.

The four assholes have finally gotten out of their cars to witness the spectacle on stage. It's far too easy to hear the doors shut. They're so fucking reckless. If we weren't bathed in chaos, every soul in Devin's pack would hear them with how loud they rush around the stadium's perimeter. I've been listening to them rant incessantly about taking back this town for the past half hour. Their voices picked up with excitement when they realized Devin and the hulking doom-and-gloom were taking mates. That's when I went from bored to pissed.

With what they joked about doing ... I'll enjoy making them suffer.

"You two go in the first car and we'll follow. As soon as we get a chance, we'll grab whichever one we can. We only need one to bring to Alpha." My eyes roll at their piss-poor plan. Haven't they seen the size of the werewolves they're so desperate to fuck with? They truly are idiots.

I don't know much about the pack of Shadow Falls, but I know enough. Devin, the current Alpha, has always belonged here. A few years ago, he left before returning with a new pack to reclaim this territory as his. He had the backing of the Authority, and he's the one the coven wants to deal with. So the "rightful pack" can piss off.

The wolf girl shrieks yet again and it pierces my eardrums, making me wince. She needs to get her shit together. I look to the stage to see the Alpha mate passed out in Devin's arms. My perfectly plucked eyebrows arch in surprise. I didn't take her to be one to faint.

"I hope we get the blond one; she looks like fun." My attention is drawn back to these four dumb fucks. Devin doesn't need to deal with this.

As I right from my seat, I imagine he'll be thanking me if I intervene and our negotiations will start out with the coven having the upper hand. He'll owe us greatly for ensuring the safety of his mate and her friend. His pack will be more willing to hear the wishes of my coven.

And from the way these dogs have been talking, it'll be my pleasure to handle this minor mess for Devin. My lips curl up into a fiendish smile. Pride flows through me as I stride toward the parking lot to take care of this little problem. Taking one last glance over my shoulder, I'm certain my wolf will search for me. He's eager and if I'm honest with myself, so am I.

CHAPTER 3

VINCE

Tossing the cloak in the trash, I'm clad in dark washed jeans and a gray hoodie as I stalk around the back of the stadium. It's mostly empty now so I can move around without being seen more easily. At the entrance to the stadium, I catch my mate's sweet scent. My chest rises and falls with a slow beat, inhaling the soft fragrance. A heat spreads along my skin and my hands flex ... *fuck*, my mouth waters even more.

I walk slowly to the gate, my boots crunching over small rocks on the pavement, and inhale deeply, taking in the faint aroma of jasmine. Relief floods through me. The gnawing pit in my stomach subsides and my skin tingles with excitement. A wolfish grin graces my lips; the hunt is on. Unfortunately, the relief is fleeting as I follow the floral breeze to the parking lot. My heartbeat picks up once again. The thought of her getting into her car and leaving me forever is a real possibility. With my inner wolf howling in protest, my pace quickens. Staying quiet and crouched in the shadows of the building, I need to stay inconspicuous. There aren't many people lingering, but I don't want to draw any attention.

I'm already too tall, my eyes not quite right. I don't fit in but I don't stand out too much either. Still, I'm careful to stick to the shadows and remain quiet.

The scent trail takes me to a few parked cars, but then it continues past the lot and toward campus. Her sweet smell cuts off to the right down a sidewalk between two dorms. My head tilts as I eye the large brick buildings. Maybe she's a student. My lips kick up into an asymmetric grin. Stalking past campus and toward Main Street, I'm eager to learn more about my mate. There are a few shops just now closing down, but there's a bar and a nightclub at the end of the street. I follow my tantalizing mate and that's when I go on high alert. Scenting the air, I fight the urge to growl.

Wolves are here. And they sure as fuck aren't from my pack. Adrenaline floods my veins knowing the trail to my mate and the trail to the unknown werewolves lead in the same direction. Both panic and anger consume me.

"Devin, we have problems." Not waiting for a response, I continue along the path. My focus narrows; my pulse

accelerates. They better not fucking touch her. I'll kill them. They will die slow deaths if they dare to approach her. Woods to my left offer a modicum of cover, allowing me to sprint. No more of this plodding human pace. I'm barely able to keep my composure until I'm safely hidden in the shadows of the forest.

I try calling for the pack again, but it's too late. They've traveled too far and can't hear me. *Fuck!* Rushing past the trees, branches snap loudly under my boots. I don't care about stealth, only speed. I need to get to her as fast as I can. If they're after my mate, I'll rip their throats out. I refuse to fail my mate. To hell with that shit about waiting until she's offered. I'm taking her with me and Devin will just have to deal with it. It only takes minutes to reach the end of her scent but with each second that passes, the growl deep in my chest gets louder. The trail cuts past the bar and through a deserted alley.

VERONICA

Time passes far too quickly as the pack trails me, and the sun sinks into the night's embrace. I almost lost sight of my little wolf stalker. The other dogs call him Vince. His name sends a chill down my spine in the most unexpected ways. The shiver of delight, of intrigue even, perks up my lips into a pleasant smile.

I love the way his silver eyes follow me, just like the lost puppy he is. My smile widens, threatening to expose my sharp fangs if I don't contain myself. How could I resist this, though? How could I resist *him?* Especially given that I've been so damn bored scouting out this Podunk town for the coven. Hearing him pant with lust dripping from his desperate whimper for me to be his has my cold, dead heart beating with scalding hot blood.

The other werewolves shadowing him have put a damper on my intrigue. Just the thought of them, of a pack, forces the pull I feel toward Vince to quiet itself. I wonder if he knows they've been tracking him all night. Probably not, considering that he hasn't stopped following my every step in these gray suede pumps. The dogs may have a better sense of smell than us vamps, but their hearing is shit.

Every pump of their hearts, every swallow, every murmur and whisper ... I hear it all. My eyes narrow with contempt at the pack following the lone wolf who's set his sights on me.

Tapping my sharp nails against the railing to the nightclub, I admire my bloodred manicure as I wait for Vince to catch up. I've done this all day, allowing the hours to pass and standing by for the sun to slip away. What's about to happen shouldn't be done in the daylight with humans out and about. The scant two hours Vince muttered about possessing have long since passed.

I could play this game of cat and mouse all day, but now that the humans have mostly dispersed, the time has come to end this charade.

The club is the only place open this late, and even it's going to close down soon. Aptly named Allure, music blares from the doors every time they open and patrons pour in and out. Tipsy women who dared to wear heels pass me with slurred speech and an unsteady gait.

I keep mulling over the words whispered by my pup's predators: *rightful pack*. The wretched creatures were planning on stealing the Alpha's new mate. Devin's mate. My crimson lips that match my nails kick up into a smirk once again. Their plan went to shit when their cars wouldn't start and they ended up stuck in this boring-ass town. Reaching into my studded black leather clutch, I pull out two spark plugs and toss them into a dingy trash can on the deserted sidewalk. The clunk ricochets down the alley, almost in rhythm with the sound of their steps coming closer and closer.

Initially I thought about cutting their brake lines, but they were planning on following my pup's pack and I wasn't sure how that would turn out. I wanted to play with him after all, and I wasn't about to let some rent-a-pack pricks wreck my night.

Wiping a touch of engine grease down the side of the brick wall, I walk slowly, not stalking, simply waiting. Contro is divine. And tonight, every bit of control is mine. My heels click against the broken asphalt beneath me as I wait, my pace turning slower and slower.

I perk up as I hear the sound of the "rightful pack" to my right. A sarcastic huff leaves me as they say it again. "Rightful pack." My long lashes flutter shut as I listen close. My pup's shuffling somewhere behind me, maybe a mile back on my left, no doubt following my scent. It seems his enemies have a new target. My smirk morphs into an all-out grin. All their muttering makes it sound like they've set their sights on me this time.

"He must be following his mate."

"Get her first."

"We'll use her to get to him. And then him to get to the pack."

Oh, those sweet foolish men. My fangs peek out ever so slightly as I bite down on my bottom lip, grateful they've finally put two and two together. How adorable that it only took them hours and not days. I can only hope Vince's pack, the one Devin has sovereignty over, isn't full of idiots like this one is.

Humming, I tap absently at the railing before piercing my nail through the metal and gouging a long scratch into it as I walk to the end of the bar. The odds are low they know I'm a vampire. Their hastily arranged plan is careless. With the element of surprise on my side, it'll be easy for me to take each one of them on my own. It's been too damn long since I've been able to release this pent-up energy. And so much longer since I've been able to drink my fill. My tongue grazes the sharp fang slightly puncturing my bottom lip.

To my right is a dark alley. The pack waits there, the ones who are determined to get revenge by scooping up their enemies' mates. My eyes roll at their pathetic plan.

To my left is a winding dirt road sheltered in a dense forest. My panting pup chose to take that route so I wouldn't see him following me around, the silly little thing. Well ... not so little.

When these werewolves meet up, I'm sure blood will be shed. Four on one isn't the best odds for my pup, although I'm interested in seeing how he'd fare. We're in human territory, though. My lips purse at the thought; the coven will be pissed if I allow it. Not to mention the Authority.

I've never been much for the outdoors and seeing as how I'm in heels, I think I'll head to my right. I wanted to have a little fun tonight anyway.

The only thing I'm not quite sure of is how much fun I'll get to have before my pup catches up to me.

VINCE

The alley is narrow and my clothing snags on the rough brick as I rush through to the other end. Hastily emerging from the shadows, my hoodie's torn to shreds so I rip it off and leave it. The white Henley stretched tight across my chest has a small tear running across my abs and is stained with blood. That's what I get from running recklessly through the wooded trails. I've already healed, though, and I don't give a fuck. The scowl on my face, clenched fists, and white-hot anger pouring off me in waves complete the image of a pissed-the-fuck-off werewolf. If I could contain my anger to avoid scaring my mate I would, but I can't. Four large frames are arranged in a loose semicircle at the end of the alley.

They have her surrounded.

I've never felt fear like I do now. Even more so, I've never felt rage as I do now.

My fists clench so hard that the skin on my knuckles tears and blood seeps from the self-induced wounds. A low growl of warning rips through my chest, reverberating in the air. All four of them lift their heads immediately, their eyes widening and mouths parting in either shock or an attempt to speak.

I don't give the fuckers a chance to say a damn thing.

As I hurl my body toward them, I release my wolf, morphing into a beast of violence. Bones contort; fur emerges. The burning sensation and cracking in my ears fuel my desire to destroy. I'm fully wolf before all four paws land on the cold, hard ground. Snarling, I'm only vaguely aware of how this may frighten my mate. This isn't how I'd planned on meeting her, on telling her who I am and what she means to me.

Regret doesn't have a moment to linger. For now, I allow the fury to consume every thought and action, consequences be dammed. One of the four assholes attempts to shift, but he's too slow as I immediately go for his throat. His claws dig into my shoulders, slicing through the tender flesh and scraping at the bone as my jaws sink into his throat, piercing his jugular and causing hot gushes of dirty blood to fill my mouth. I barely feel a damn thing. A low snarl leaves me as his body goes limp and I turn to the other three.

My eyes flicker with shock and then pride as I take in the scene. My sexy mate's knees are crossed with her thighs wrapped around the neck of a man who must be human judging by his inability to shift. I don't have time to question what a human is doing with these werewolves as she flings her body toward the ground, silently and effortlessly. Tossing his large frame in the air, he lands hard on his back with her sitting on his chest. The crack of his bones echoes in the alley as she peeks up at me.

Holy fuck.

My gaze is locked on her as she lashes at his throat, slicing it with a small knife nestled between her knuckles. Her expression is that of a ruthless predator. Her perfectly pinned bun has fallen, leaving her black curls to cascade gently down her back. Confidence and power radiate from her small frame as she turns, still crouched on his chest. Her dark red, plump lips part as she lifts her head and hisses at the remaining shifters.

revealing long white fangs that reflect the light of the moon.

The shifters stumble back, mouths gaped, but before they're able to turn and run she quickly flings her hand outward, sending two blades flying. The first lands in one man's back, effectively paralyzing him and his limp body instantly sinks to the ground, crashing against the cement. With nothing to break his fall, blood flows freely from his broken nose, pooling around his face. The other blade is lodged in the last shifter's neck. As his hands fly up to his neck, my mate, my *vampire* mate, sends more blades darting through the air in a rhythmic dance, pinning his hands to the base of his throat. Blood spurts from his jugular. The sight is violent and bloody, brutal and efficient. As the shifter struggles to breathe, landing hard on his knees and coughing up blood, my mate saunters over casually and twists the knives while ripping them out. His dead eyes stare at nothing as blood forms a puddle around him and his face flattens against the brick.

Noticeably catching her breath, her chest rises and falls and I'm given a moment to admire her. A vampire. My mate is paranormal, not human. There will be so much less to explain.

With dark red blood splattered on her blouse, her heels click as she strides to the other shifter, who's limp yet conscious. With my hackles settling, I prowl closer, but give her the room she obviously desires. Squatting, my gaze is captured by her leather skirt sliding up her leg, revealing a black lacy garter belt holding up her thigh highs. She is the sight of deadly beauty. Still in wolf form, I groan with lust and desire. I move to shift, but her dark eyes find mine and her lips part as she says,

"Stay. I want to feel you ... like this. I want to see you up close."

If I could grin, I would. She'll know damn well how much hearing that pleased me the moment I shift. Pride flows through me and I huff in agreement as I pad over swiftly to be closer to her. Her delicate hand grabs the knife, but before retrieving it she looks back at me. "I thought we could keep him for Devin." Although it's a statement, it's clear she's asking me. My hackles raise, realizing she knows more of me than I know of her. She waits for my nod and then she removes the knife. It's a silver blade. He'll heal with time, but we'll deal with him before he has a chance to come to. I watch her skilled moves while coming to terms with the situation. My mate is a vampire and she knows of Devin. Numerous questions pile in my mind, but in wolf form I'm unable to speak. Standing, she places the bloody blade behind her back and tilts her head as she takes me in.

Her dark eyes travel down my body. Although she's shorter than I am, we're the same height while I'm standing on all four paws in my wolf form.

"Lie down." Her command makes me grin inwardly. I'm so fucking turned on it hurts. I need to shift so I can play this game with her. Obeying my mate, I settle on the ground in the brick alley. A low rumble vibrates my chest as she spears my fur with her small hands, petting me. She moves in front of me and takes my large head in her grasp before gently scratching my chest. Her touch on me is a heaven I didn't know existed. I resist the urge to close my eyes so I can stare back at her while enjoying her touch. A small smile plays at her lips as she watches her fingers disappear in my thick, soft fur. All too quickly, she stops. Her smile vanishes as she glances at the bodies around her.

She purses her lips and looks behind us at my tattered and shredded outfit. "You ruined your clothes." I sit up, making me about a foot taller than her so I tower over her, but she maintains eye contact. "What are you going to wear now?" Is she admonishing me? "I'm going to need help moving these bodies and storing him in the trunk." Her thumb points to the incapacitated shifter. "I have silver rope in the back of the car, but how the hell am I going to carry him?" Her tongue clucks as she surveys the scene. "You need clothes. Do you have any?" I shake my head, causing her dark eyes to narrow. "Shift."

My mate is ... testing me. I allow a moment to pass, observing her and she stares back at me, her confidence disappearing for only a moment. "Please," she adds, dragging out the word as if she's not used to saying it.

That's better. All I can think before I shift back is that my mate is going to challenge me, push me, command me even ... and I'm eager to play and to do the same in return.

CHAPTER 4

VINCE

Tossing her keys on the bedside table in the hotel room, I perk up as I hear the shower being turned on. I buried the human and the two shifters in the woods after tying up the remaining one with silver rope and locking him in Veronica's trunk. Her name was the first thing I requested. I can't get over the way the four syllables roll off my tongue.

Time was short between us, though, with barely any words spoken other than a hastily devised plan. Bury the three, throw the other in the back of her trunk and then lie low at this hotel.

After all of that, a shower is desperately needed and then I have to call Devin. He needs to know everything and more importantly, that we have a shifter roped in silver to interrogate.

The fucker pissed all over himself, but he'll live. For now. I don't know how long that'll last once Devin finds out what they were planning.

I strip out of the jeans and simple white T-shirt my mate got me. The shirt barely fits, but I think she likes seeing it stretched tight across my broad shoulders. She knew damn well I needed a larger size.

So far I've learned my mate is opinionated. She likes what she likes, and I'm hard as a fucking rock for her. Every little detail about her seems to scream to me to pay attention. From the way a soft accent lingers on a few of her words, to the way she tucks her jet-black hair behind her ear to accentuate her slender neck. I crave every inch of her.

Every step I take toward the bathroom makes my dick harder as I imagine my gorgeous mate wet and naked, waiting for me to ravage her. Palming myself, I stroke a few times.

The bathroom door opens with a soft creak, allowing the steam to billow out and I find her wrapped in a towel. Her hair's dry and she's rubbing some balm that smells like honey into her shoulders. There's a large dark bruise covering the crook of her neck and the sight of it makes me growl deep and low.

They hurt her. I was right fucking there and they laid hands on her. Weakness and anger war within me. I was right there and I didn't protect her. The bastard in the trunk is lucky that she wants to give him to Devin. If it were up to me, he'd be dead like the rest of them. I know vampires heal, but obviously they don't heal as fast as we do.

"Vince." My name on her lips pulls my attention from my dark thoughts.

"Don't be so upset, pup. It's just a little bruise." Her dark eyes twinkle with mischief when they meet my silver gaze in the mirror.

Pup. If I wasn't feeling as if I've failed her already, only hours into meeting my mate, I'd smirk at her nickname for me. *Pup.* I imagine once she discovers what I can do to her, she won't be using that word anymore.

As it is, my gaze falls back to the bruise. "I don't like to see you marked."

She smiles devilishly before turning around and unwrapping her towel. The white cotton falls to form a puddle around her feet, revealing her light brown skin that looks flawless.

Peeking over her shoulder, she toys with me. "You don't want to put your mark on me then?"

I groan in approval. My dick gets impossibly harder and lust rages in my blood at the sight of her gorgeous curves. *My mate.* I part my lips to speak as I walk toward her, but she stops me by putting one slender finger against my lips. "Uh, uh, uh. I want my big bad wolf on his knees." Smirking, I obey my mate. I love this little game. Just the thought of her putting a collar and leash on me makes precum leak from my slit. She can do what she pleases as I learn her boundaries.

"You want me to lick you first?" I question.

I kneel in front of her and gently place my hands on the back of her thighs, petting her smooth skin and testing my limits. She allows it and I smile up at her in gratitude before nuzzling my nose between her thighs and inhaling her arousal. She's wet already. Wanting me as much as I want her. My groan matches the desire in her moan. She leans back against the counter, spreading her legs a little wider. "Good boy. Enjoy your treat."

I can't help but to grin against her pussy. *Pup. Good boy. Kneel.* If she wants to be in control, who am I to turn down a good time? Besides, it's enticing. I've never met a woman like her. I've never craved this like I do now.

A rough chuckle vibrates through my chest and I smile into her heat before taking a long, languid lick through her lips. *Fuck.* She tastes just like honey too. Moaning into her heat, I suck on her clit. I massage her with my hot tongue and pick up my pace as she mewls louder and runs her hands through my hair. My tongue dips between her folds and I lap up her honey. I pull back to look at her glistening opening before shoving my tongue deep inside her and she bucks against me. I'd smile at her arousal but I don't want to let up tongue fucking her.

My hands grip onto her thighs to hold her tighter as she starts to tremble, already close as her breathing picks up, my fingers digging into her skin. I pull away to run my tongue along her length and suck her clit back into my mouth before she can protest. Her small hands push me against her.

I slow my movements as she gets closer to her release, her thighs tightening as she holds her breath. I want to hear her beg me to get her off. I want this sexy-as-fuck, dominant woman to beg me for her release. She moans my name and pushes me into her harder. My name. My name is what she pleads for.

She may be greedy, but I'm full of pride. I suck her clit back into my mouth but slow my movements as her hands shake in my hair and her pussy clenches. Imagining her body shuddering in my arms while her orgasm rocks through her makes me leak more precum onto the bathroom floor. Impossibly hard, I want nothing more than to push her against the wall and fuck her so I can feel her come on my dick. I stop my movements as she moans my name louder. I grin before taking another languid stroke against her wanting heat.

Her heavy breathing slows and her hands grip my hair tighter to the point of pain. She forces me to look up at her. Her narrowed gaze is heated. "Do you enjoy teasing me?"

"I want you to beg me." My simple statement makes her grin.

"I don't beg." She releases my head and walks to the

shower, which is still running. The shower is filled with so much steam she nearly vanishes as she steps into the glass stall. She doesn't shut the door, though, and the steam flows out into the room, giving me a better view. "Come here."

My gaze narrows but I immediately oblige.

"Everyone begs," I tell her. My head tilts, waiting to see if she's serious. Her hand reaches out and her splayed fingers push against my chest before I can join her. The hot sprays of water splash against her chest, reddening her skin. "Knees." My brow furrows, but I do what she says and kneel on the small white bath mat.

"I don't take it lightly that you didn't let me get off." Her admonishing tone sends a pulse of nervousness through my chest. She closes her eyes and lets the water hit her face and hair before streaming over her lush curves. "Now you'll have to watch." She opens her eyes and faces me before cupping my chin in her hand. "I wanted to let you pleasure me ..." Her pitying voice turns stern as she continues, "... but I don't need you to get mine."

Her cold words crater my chest. My lips press into a hard line. I don't fucking like this. "No." It's the only word that will escape my lips, my growl of contempt barely restrained as I speak.

"You did this to yourself." She watches me through her thick lashes. "Take your punishment like a good boy and I'll reward you." She pats my head before adding, "I'm willing to believe you didn't know any better."

My fists clench at my sides to hold back from grabbing her waist, pushing her small body against the wall and pounding into her tight pussy. I could easily take her however I wanted, and she knows it. She's taunting a beast, trying to tame me.

The moment is tense between us and I know she feels it too from the way her expression changes. A second passes and then another. "A good boy?"

"I need to be the one in charge, Vince," she tells me with her voice tight. "If that's not going to work, you—"

"Fine." I cave before she can say another word. There's something off about her, something ill at ease and frightened. But more importantly, she wants me. My mate, the only soul I'm meant to be with. "You want to call the shots?"

"I want you to do everything I say and nothing more." With a second passing in silence, her long black hair slicked to her tan skin, her breasts taut and this dangerous woman vulnerable before me, she adds, "I'll be good to you but this is how I need it."

There is more. I'm certain of it. But for now, I ease her worries. We have a lifetime to spend together. And I don't mind playing the part of whatever she needs in this role.

I grin and sit back on my heels, then say, "Yes, ma'am." She smiles brightly, looking down at me with delight in her dark eyes that fills a void I've held in my chest for all my life.

"Call me Mistress." I nearly come on the damn rug at her

words. Stifling my groan, I regain my composure.

"Yes, Mistress." My obedience makes her sharp fangs sink into her pouty bottom lip. The sight makes me want to beg her to bite me. Shit. Maybe some part of me wants to be her submissive. I want her to pierce my skin, marking me just as I plan on marking her.

Her fingers dip into her heat and she throws her head back, moaning at her own tender touch. She tilts her head to look at me with her fingers strumming along her clit. "You got me so close." Her cadence is soft and full of yearning.

"Can I taste ... Mistress?" My question makes her lips kick up into a smile. Her happiness fills my heart with pride. She offers me her fingers and I reach out a hand to hold them steady, but she pulls them away before I can touch her.

"Only taste." She shakes her head, sending droplets of water down her breasts to the tips of her dark brown nipples before landing on the rug. "No touching." Her mouth is parted slightly and her breasts rise and fall with her deep breaths. The smell of her arousal floods the bathroom. I place my hands on my thighs and lean forward. Giving her a wolfish grin, I stare into her dark eyes as I take her fingertips into my mouth to taste her honey. I let out a groan at the taste and sit back on my heels.

"Fucking delicious."

She smiles with satisfaction and returns to touching herself. Her head leans back against the stall as she moans her clit and dip into her entrance over and over. I watch her n rapture as she brings herself to the edge of her climax. Her mouth gapes and her shoulders spasm as she finds her release. She screams out my name before sagging against the wall of the shower.

My name.

It's the most beautiful vision I've ever seen. Sitting patiently on my heels with my hands firmly pressed against my thighs, I wait for her to come down from the aftershocks. I wish I was holding her and she had gotten off on my tongue. Next time. Her next orgasm will be mine.

As if she read my mind, she backs up against the tiled wall and beckons me into the shower with a playful smirk. Rising slowly, I carefully navigate my large frame into the shower, crowding the space and hovering over her tiny body. She takes my face in her hands and I lower my lips to hers. My tongue brushes along the seam of her lips and she parts them for me, her hot tongue massaging mine. I growl into her mouth and rest my forearms on either side of her head against the wall, caging her in as I kiss her with every ounce of passion I have. Her arms wrap around my waist, her fingers splayed against my ass, pulling me closer to her. She breaks our kiss and moans a contented sigh as my erection digs into her soft belly. Ducking her head and stepping under my arm, she reaches for a small bottle of body wash.

"Have you learned your lesson?" She lathers the soap in her hands before massaging it over my body. Her fingers linger over my chiseled chest and play in the small bit of hair below my abs, trailing down to my cock. I nod and tell her, "Yes."

She makes a sound like she's pleased and stands on her tiptoes to kiss the crook of my neck. "Good boy." Her hot breath tickles my throat as her sharp fangs skim along the sensitive flesh. She hastily turns away from me and applies more soap to her hands. Twirling a finger, she commands me to turn. Her hands knead my muscles as she lathers more soap onto my skin. Every little touch from her is heaven. My mate. I'm still in awe.

She hums as she washes every inch of my body *except* my raging erection.

My mate is a fucking tease.

At that realization she commands, "Turn."

I obey slowly, turning to face her. She gets onto her tiptoes to wash my hair, her breasts pressing against my hard chest. Fuck, I love it though. My arms wrap around her small waist as she massages my scalp with her nails. Her touch relaxes me.

"You like calling me pup?" I ask her, planting a small kiss on her temple.

Her smile is soft and playful. "You're at least a foot taller than me ... I think I love calling you pup."

Love. She's demanding, controlling and there's a reason for

he way she is ... but she wants to be with me. To be my mate.
She offers no protest at all and I know damn well she knows
what this means. "Do you like it?" she questions in a whisper.

"Mmm." I murmur into the crook of her neck as I grind
my dick into her stomach, loving the skin-on-skin contact.
The touch reminds me how much I fucking need my release.
She lets out a small, feminine snicker, but otherwise ignores
my not-so-subtle hint.

She steps toward the back of the shower and instructs me
to rinse. I chuckle, loving the way she orders me around like
she owns me. She really fucking does own me. What's worse
is that she knows it. I let the hot water hit me and rinse the
suds from my body, but I don't linger. I want my mate. I
need more of her touch. With a single stride toward her, I
cage her in like before. I move to kiss her soft, supple lips, but
her finger at my mouth stops me inches away from her face.
"Bedtime, wolf." *Bed.* Absolutely.

"Yes, Mistress." My response is paired with a grin and I
lean forward to kiss her cheek. A blush runs through her
chest and up to her face. The slight pink hue looks beautiful
on her olive complexion. I dry off as quickly as possible and
the soft cotton against my still-hard dick is enough to have
me on my knees. God, I can't wait to get off. Hopefully it'll
be in her tight little cunt. I lick my lips, remembering the
mouthwatering taste.

She seems to be taking her time towel drying her hai

before she reaches in a small floral bag on the counter and pulls out lotion. When my silver eyes catch her dark gaze in the mirror, I cock a brow. "I'll be there when I'm finished." I nod my head, not trusting that my mouth won't demand she come with me if I open it. Fuck, I'm tired of waiting. Tired of being teased. I lie on top of the covers with my hands behind my head, looking at the bathroom. I left the door open and I keep getting hints of her honey scent mingling with the sweet, floral fragrance of jasmine.

She saunters to the bed completely naked and it makes my dick snap to attention. She smirks at the sight of my bobbing erection before climbing into bed, pulling up the covers and crawling underneath. "Get under here. I want you to hold me." I move as quickly as I can to get my hands on her lush body. My arms reach around her waist and pull her small, delicate frame to my hard chest. I rock my dick into her ass, and even that feels like heaven.

"Stop it. I don't want you to do that." Her softly spoken words shock me, but I immediately stop. My brow furrows as she nuzzles her head into my chest, drapes her leg across mine and settles her forearm across my abs. She's getting into position to sleep. "Good night, pup." *What the fuck?* My lips part to protest but that damn finger comes up to silence me yet again. "Uh-uh. No complaining. You kept me from my release to tease me ... for your own pleasure. Bad boys don't get to come." She settles back into my chest as I contemplate her words.

A tic in my jaw spasms, but then a thought comes to mind. "Are you challenging me?"

Her gentle snicker tickles my chest hair, then she says, "No, not in the least. I know if you wanted to, you could take from me. I don't want that." I didn't think she was, but I had to make sure. Tapping my fingers on her arm, I try to figure out what the hell I should do. A fucking lightbulb goes off in my head.

"Do you want me to beg?" Of course she does. I wanted her to beg, so this is my punishment. "I'll beg on my knees. I'll plead with you. Whatever you want." I whisper my words into her hair, meaning every word. Shit, just the thought of me begging her to suck me off has precum flowing down my shaft.

She snickers again and I know her answer before she says it. "No, I don't want you to beg."

"I don't like this." I know I sound like a petulant child, but really, what the fuck?

"That's the point of a punishment." She lifts her head to give me a kiss on the cheek before settling back down beside me. A moment of silence passes. I stare up at the ceiling with a raging erection that won't die, next to my sated mate, who doesn't seem to have any intention of returning the favor. *Motherfucker.* I close my eyes and try to sleep, but there's no fucking way that's going to happen.

"Vince, I'm thirsty." Her sleepy words register slowly.

"You need to drink? Do you have any blood here?"

Vampires don't drink directly from beings anymore. At least they aren't supposed to; it was bad for *relations*. Her head shakes gently, ruffling her hair before she nips at my neck. Her little bite shoots a wave of heated desire down my body.

"Will it hurt?" If I'd known my mate was going to be a vampire, I would have given more of a shit about their species.

"Only a little," she says and hesitates before adding, "at first." I nod once and arch my neck, offering it to her without thinking twice. She straddles my body and her naked, hot core presses down on my tortured erection, making my eyes roll back in my head. *Fuck yes!*

"Drink it all, baby." The lustful words slip past my lips as she licks my neck, telling me where she's going to bite.

"Stay still." She breathes into my neck. "Just feel it." I barely register her words before her sharp fangs pierce my flesh. It stings and I have to fist the sheets to keep my hands from instinctively going to my neck. And then she sucks. *Holy fuck.* I can feel the pull of my blood through my veins. The intense rush is accompanied with a heated pulse of pleasure hovering over every inch of me. I groan and tighten my grip on the sheets. She rocks gently on top of me while sucking harder and I almost come from the heightened sensation. My legs stiffen with the need to release.

"More." It's not even close to a command, but before I can add *please* she digs her fangs in deeper and sucks harder. And I erupt. The tingling in my spine travels through every inch of my body, starting at my toes and fingers and numbing its way through my quivering body. Waves and waves of cum leave me as she continues to suck on my neck, intensifying my release. As aftershocks flow through me, she gently licks the bite wounds. The soft touch sends a satisfied chill through my body. She shuffles onto the bed beside me and kisses me tenderly on the lips before grabbing something off the nightstand. Wiping herself with a damp cloth, she then scoots over to clean off my stomach and thighs.

"You made a mess." Her voice is teasing, as is her side-eye.

Her weak admonishment makes me grin and I tell her, "You knew I would." She gives me a soft, small smile and continues wiping me down before tossing the rag on the floor.

"Did I taste good?" I have to ask.

"Delicious." She answers with my own words before nipping at my neck and settling beside me.

"Did you even drink enough?"

She hums into my chest while molding her soft warm body to mine. "Sleep."

"Yes, my little mate."

"That's not how you say Mistress." I feel her smile as her deep breaths even out and she nods off.

CHAPTER 5

VERONICA

I'm impressed, and that's a rarity. My sharp nail taps against my lower lip while taking in the view. Appraising it. The pack's estate is massive and modernized. I wasn't sure what would await me, but this has certainly exceeded my expectations.

Just like my big bad wolf. I clench my thighs in anticipation. I haven't decided how long I'm going to make him wait. I do know I'm enjoying the tease far too much to give in.

He isn't going to hurt me, though. I've been trained all my life to kill. I've been hurt more than my fair share. But Vince, whether it's because I'm his mate or it's simply who he is, isn't going to do a damn thing to hurt me.

Clearing my throat, I check my composure in the

reflection of the garage window. Covens and packs have treaties and the Authority has strict laws so I'm protected, theoretically, walking into the wolves' den.

I would have felt more secure on human territory, but now that I know what I mean to Vince, that certainly changes things. I don't appreciate the anxiousness it offers me.

As my patience wanes, I hear my pup hurl the limp body of the shifter bound with silver rope onto the paved driveway with a loud thud.

A wicked grin spreads across my face as I listen in on the heated conversation flowing from the windows as two sets of footsteps come down the stairs. It may be faint to these mutts, but I can hear just fine. "I need it, Devin." The Alpha mate is practically seething. Usually I try not to eavesdrop, but I can't help the fact that the angry human is fighting with her mate. Although she's whispering, she's furious. I wonder what her wolf has done to piss her off.

"You're my mate. You're meant to carry my pups." My eyebrows shoot up at his response. I can feel the low, threatening growl barreling from his chest. His mate's response is even and firm. "I need my birth control." Pursing my lips, I listen more intently but am unfortunately interrupted.

"What's wrong?" My sweet pup looks devilishly handsome as he wraps his arm around my waist and kisses my cheek. I lean into his touch slightly, but hold back.

"Have you already told them?"

"Yes, they know everything. They're gathering now to meet you." I nod in acknowledgment. An odd sense of discomfort settles through me. It's been a while since I've felt this way, but I think I'm genuinely nervous. I huff as the realization hits me. Shaking my head, I shut that shit down as I strut in my suede pumps toward the entrance with my pup following closely behind. When I get to the door I pause, waiting for him to open it for me, which he does easily.

My big bad wolf is such a gentleman. He leads me through the expansive hall toward the eat-in kitchen with his large hand resting on the small of my back. I square my shoulders as I enter the room and see the other seven members of the pack staring back at me.

"Veronica, this is my pack. Caleb, Liz, Dom, Grace, Devin, Lev and Jude." He motions toward each of them as he says their names and they nod in turn. Both Liz and Grace look uncomfortable at my presence and it causes a chill to go through me. I restrain myself from sneering at their obvious distaste for my species. Or maybe it's just a dislike for me. Either way, I don't care for the immediate judgment. Although I'm used to it. I offer them a curt nod each.

Caleb and Dom are on either side of their mate on the left side of the table with the Alpha mate, Grace, next to Dom. Her small muscles are corded as she eyes me. A knowing smirk pulls at my lips. The little human is balling her fists under the table. It's difficult not to laugh. I have to remind myself that she knows little of vampires. Whatever small bits of knowledge she's been given have almost certainly been designed to cause fear. Devin is seated next to her at the head of the table and the other two pack members are on his right.

"Hello." I greet them all at once, making eye contact with each of them as I take a seat at the opposite end of the table without hesitation. Vince pulls out my chair and scoots it in as I sit before joining me at my right. His affection toward me gives me confidence I wasn't expecting. I'm growing rather fond of him, far too quickly. So much so that I don't trust it. I know of mates and werewolves, but this ... these feelings are uncontrollable. I don't care for them.

The large wolf to the right of Devin smiles at me and asks, "Do you know the difference between ooh and aah?" The wolf next to him smacks him in the back of the head.

"Shut it, Lev." The large wolf chuckles, unaffected by the hit.

"About ten inches," I answer effortlessly with a straight face. I rather enjoy crude humor. Most of the pack laughs and Lev gapes, though there's a twinkle of camaraderie in his eyes. It earns him a small smile in return. Grace's cold gaze narrows and Liz continues to shy away, hiding behind Caleb. I make a mental note to mention a coffee run and a trip to the pharmacy before the conversation is over. They'll be begging me to come along. A wicked grin curls up my lips.

I'm not the monster here; they'll learn that. Monsters and evil exist, but that's not who I am.

"I welcome you to our pack," Devin begins, although I hear an unspoken *but*.

"Thank you."

"Why were you in our territory?" Devin's baritone voice is even and disrupts my thoughts.

"I respect your straightforwardness." Meeting his silver eyes with a professional gaze, I begin. "As you know, with the new laws, our food source is now scarce. We're doing our best to respect the Authority's wishes, but the blood banks are hardly providing enough to sustain us."

"Your coven sent you?"

"Yes."

"Just you?"

"Yes; there are no others. I was hoping to talk after the offering on human territory, for obvious reasons."

The pack nods in unison at that comment. They wouldn't dare cause a scene in front of humans. Not when it means facing the consequences of the Authority. "I didn't anticipate the ..." I pause and tap my bloodred fingernails along the table thinking of an acceptable word. "... distractions."

"What distractions?" Grace speaks up. It seems her curiosity is greater than her fear. There's hope for us after all.

"Well, you fainting for one." She pales at the reminder. "And Liz screaming certainly wasn't conducive to holding a business meeting." I eye the petite blonde, who has yet to smile. "It seems you're both much more agreeable today."

There's only a thin veil of sarcasm over my words. "And then of course ... the dogs."

"Vince has informed us. You have my sincerest gratitude." I can't help but to smile at the Alpha's warmth.

"He's in the shed." Vince leans back in his seat. "All set up for questioning." I eye my pup with envy. He's laid back and easygoing.

How fate has matched us, I have no idea. I don't know what he did in some other life to be stuck with a woman like me. Guarded and quite honestly, vengeful. I almost feel sorry for him that I'm the woman who's meant to love him. I think I've long forgotten how to do such a thing.

"What dogs?" A tic in Devin's jaw spasms at Grace's question.

"We'll discuss that matter later."

The little human's discontent is palpable. Judging by the bags under her eyes, it doesn't appear that she's slept much. Poor thing. Absently, I wonder how she's taking all of this in. Glancing to Liz, I gather Grace is faring better, seeing as how she's at least speaking her mind. "I want to know what you're talking about." Devin faces his mate with a hard glare, but his voice is soft when he speaks. He gently takes her hands in his. "Later, sweetheart. I will tell you later."

Her lips purse before she parts them several times without speaking. Finally, she nods her head and repeats, "Later."

He places their clasped hands on top of the table. "So you

came to discuss business matters on behalf of your coven?"

"Yes. As I was saying, the blood banks aren't enough. Our research indicates that the overwhelming majority of the Shadow Falls residents do not give blood. We're willing to pay them substantially for their donations."

"The Authority has approved this?"

"Only on the premise that it's run by humans and that they are not privy to any information involving vampires."

I pause, picking up the sound of tires on the long, winding driveway. Someone is coming. I listen closer.

"What does the coven—" I hold my hand up, interrupting Devin's question. I shouldn't have disrespected him, but I act without thinking.

"Are you expecting company?" I ask.

"No." His silver eyes narrow.

I barely hear the voice, but I instantly recognize it. Yet another distraction. Chills trail down my spine. I may not have feared a den of wolves, but I certainly fear who's coming next.

"The Authority is here."

PART II
WOLF IN PAIN

CHAPTER 6

GRACE

"Who the fuck is the Authority?"

It feels like with every turn I make, there's something new I haven't been told. Every time I try to take control, my life is ripped from my possession. This man beside me ... he's keeping things from me and I can feel it with every bit of marrow in my bones.

His jaw clenches hard at my question and I can tell he's debating on what he should say. "You told me you would tell me everything, Devin." I can barely contain my frustration as I force out the words. From the corner of my eye, I see Jude cower at my hostility to his Alpha. It almost makes me regret it. *Almost.* He says I'm his mate and therefore his equal, but he's not treating me like it.

I barely have a grip on anything, let alone any choices in these matters.

Devin seems unbothered by my tone and that pisses me off even more. "The Authority is in charge of communications between and within species. They formed an alliance with the humans and enacted laws to prevent certain instances from occurring." I narrow my eyes at his sanitized response.

"Instances such as the one that occurred yesterday at the offering." Veronica elaborates, her bewitching voice demanding my attention, the faint accent only adding to her beauty. Her tanned skin is flawless, while the way she carries herself is both demure and yet superior. I still don't know what to make of her.

She's a vampire and that alone sends up red flags. I hardly heard a word out of her mouth because every time her lips moved I could only stare at her fangs. She's provocative and the embodiment of female strength; both things I value highly, yet I find myself on guard. She has a seductive aura I don't trust.

Although she's not the only one I hesitate to trust.

"So they're like the werewolf police?"

Veronica's feminine laugh echoes in the kitchen. She smiles, revealing those sharp fangs, and tells me, "The Authority looks out for themselves, first and foremost. Very little of what they do involves justice."

"They can be very just in their actions, Veronica." Devin's response is slightly reprimanding.

"Just because they can be doesn't mean they have been. They often choose a route that will instill fear and maintain their position in power. Would you not agree?"

Vince cocks a brow at his mate and her tone. Rather than overriding her, as Devin's done to me, he smirks, nodding slightly and waiting for Devin's response.

"At times." He concedes as his hand finds mine under the table.

That feels far more like equality than "hush now, I'll fill you in later."

The fact that she is Vince's mate is the only reason I'm not terrified of her. Devin assured me. Hell, maybe I do trust him. I don't know what to think about anything anymore.

"I'm certain they're here because of last night." Veronica nods her head in agreement and runs her fingernails lightly along Vince's upturned hand, almost as if she's not aware she's touching him. My heart skips a beat. I wonder if she feels this too? This overwhelming need to be with her mate like I do with Devin.

It's heady and confusing. It feels like something else is taking over my body and, if I'm being honest, it's terrifying. The word "fate" has lost the comfort it used to hold.

"What do you mean?" I'm sure he's referring to the offering, but I don't understand what it has to do with them.

Generally speaking, there isn't any resistance at the offerings. Mates go willingly. Humans hardly fight for those who don't mind being taken. You fainted after fighting me and Liz had to be carried out while she resisted and screamed."

I can feel the blood drain from my face. "Oh." I bite the inside of my cheek. They're here because they think we aren't their mates. Lizzie sulks in Caleb's arms.

"I'm certain the response to the scene has been less than pleasant on the human side of relations, which will piss off the Authority. They prefer to keep the masses content."

"They're discussing it now." Veronica stares at Vince's hand and continues running the tips of her fingers along his wrist as she speaks. "They're planning on taking them back." Her words send a jolt of anxiousness through me. I can't go back. I belong here, with Devin. Everything in me knows I'm meant to be with him. Even if we are struggling to find stable and common ground. I've barely been given a chance.

"Well, the Authority can go fuck themselves." Dom's seething baritone voice startles me, making me flinch. Devin's arm wraps around my waist and pulls me closer to him.

"There's no need to be hostile. I'm sure once they see Grace and Liz, they'll leave in peace."

"It might not be your intention, but it will end up being hostile." Veronica's eyes are still fixed on her playful touch. If she wasn't consistently speaking, I wouldn't think she was listening.

I dare to ask her, "Why's that?" I'm not leaving. The thought of never seeing Devin again makes my chest feel hollow. I won't let it happen.

Her dark eyes find mine and she gives me a small smile with her fangs digging into her full bottom lip. "Natalia's a bitch."

"How do you know Natalia?" Vince asks with curiosity. I fucking loathe that everyone knows everyone else except for me. With my complete attention, I glance between the two of them, determined to find my place and the confidence I used to have.

"She's the one who trained me." Her smile falls slightly.

"Trained you for what?"

"To kill werewolves." Devin's serious response, answering for Veronica, makes my blood run cold, causing goosebumps to run down my arms. I stare with wide eyes down the end of the table. *She kills werewolves?*

My breath leaves me and I feel light-headed.

"Times were much different back then." Her lips tilt down into a small frown before she schools her expression. "I don't participate in the sport anymore."

Vince's eyes smile with humor at the knowledge; he has no fear of his mate. He doesn't seem affected at all. He relaxes into his seat and takes her hand in his before sweetly kissing her knuckles. "Ain't fate a bitch." A soft smile plays at her lips, but her large eyes are full of pain and torture.

"You had your reasons." Devin's words are spoken with compassion and it eases my discomfort marginally. She nods slightly at Devin as a loud, melodic chime echoes in the room.

Devin inclines his head in silence and remains seated. At his nod, Jude stands up to answer the door. I watch as Dom positions Lizzie on his lap and Caleb angles his body so he's directly in front of her with his chest toward the entrance after giving her a small kiss on the cheek. He's still smiling faintly, but his silver eyes have a lethal look to them. Their defensive act puts me on edge. Devin pulls my chair closer to him and kisses my forehead before nuzzling his nose in my hair. "Everything is fine, sweetheart. They will not touch you."

"Promise me."

"Everything I tell you is a promise. My entire existence is a promise to you," he tells me and his confession is a balm, a drug. It's everything I didn't know I needed.

I close my eyes, enjoying his tender touch and when I open them the Authority, comprised of three foreboding figures, is staring back at me. My body tenses and my lungs still. The bit of soothing from Devin is powerless when I take in the intimidating trio.

There are two men and a woman, all three in black cloaks like the ones from the offering. The woman is obviously a vampire. She radiates seduction and power just as Veronica does. But her eyes are a shade darker than bloodred and there's no hint of the mischievousness that twinkles in

Veronica's brown eyes. Only wickedness exists in her gaze. Her thin lips curl up at one end, revealing a sharp fang. Her pale skin and sunken cheeks make her appear older than Veronica. Much, much older. The sight of her sends an unwanted chill down my spine.

The men are both large, similar to Devin, but not as bulky or muscular. The man on the right, carrying a large black duffle bag, has silver eyes and the crooked smile of a man not to be trusted. The one on the left is devilishly handsome with a smile that seems charming and inviting, plus the lightest blue eyes I've ever seen. The skin around his eyes wrinkles when he smiles, giving away his older age. But his dimples pull you in with a boyish charm. His presence is instantly calming, negating the fear the other two instill.

"Good afternoon." Devin is short, but cordial. His hard voice snaps me out of my daze.

"I suppose the blood on the driveway doesn't belong to your mates?" The silver-eyed man speaks first.

Every bit of me feels cold from his words. It's not a traveling chill; it happens all at once.

A low growl rumbles from Dom's chest, but Devin remains unaffected, merely cocking a brow. "We would not harm our mates. I'm sure you could smell that it's shifter blood."

"So they do in fact belong to you?" His choice of words makes me snort. They may be intimidating as all hell, but I can't help my reaction. It doesn't go unnoticed. When the cloaked fucker eyes me, I just smirk. It's slightly forced, but still. With Devin's possessive hold on me growing tighter, a sense of confidence spreads through me.

"Grace and Lizzie, meet Natalia, Remy and Alec." They each nod in turn and I give them a tight smile while they take seats at the far end of the table. It's quiet as the legs of the chairs drag across the floor. Alec and Devin seem to engage in a quiet conversation before Alec's eyes settle on Dom and his lips press into a firm, hard line.

"I see. We'll need them to give a statement. The *humans* want it to be done live," Natalia speaks with annoyance thick in her tone. "I'm so glad they rightfully belong to you. It would've been a shame to start off on such poor terms."

A nervousness pricks at my skin and the thinly veiled admission of violence brings an anger out of me, one that seems intensified. Every emotion seems to swing back and forth like a wild pendulum.

"We have an issue that needs to be attended to. Also, as you know, we've just met our mates and the claiming is only two days away. So the sooner we can get this over with, the better."

"Eager to throw us out, old friend?" Alec smiles with a light dancing in his eyes.

"I'd like to tend to my mate's needs. I'd throw out my mother if she were still alive." Caleb's humorous response gains a laugh from Alec and a huff of humor from Lev. Dom is still obviously on edge, but then again, his hard glare and scowl never seem to leave him.

"We've all had a long night getting acquainted with our mates, and familiarizing them with their new lives. We'd like to continue getting them settled as soon as possible."

"Of course. Where would you like to set up?" Devin stands. He looks down at me, still seated and offers me his hand. I place my small hand in his, taking his lead and having faith that all is well. A trace of a smile graces his lips for just a moment. The rest of the pack follows suit as he leads us to a large front room. A single pane of glass lines the side wall overlooking a forest. The view is spectacular and the sight of it reminds me that I haven't even had a tour of my new home.

I barely know anything at all.

I search the large room for Lizzie to gauge her reaction and find her small frame molded to Caleb's body. Her shoulders are hunched forward and the familiar smile I'm accustomed to is nowhere to be found. She looks utterly lost. My heart shatters at the sight of her. My bubbly, spirited best friend is shadowed by a dark cloud.

I hate this. I hate how all of this happened. Somehow, it feels as if it's my fault. Every bit of it.

"Lizzie—" I start to say as I take a step forward to go to her side, but Devin's grip tightens, halting my movement. He leans down to whisper in my ear.

"Not now." I grit my teeth and prepare to shove him

way, but Lizzie catches my eyes and smiles at me. It's not a weak smile, but not quite a happy smile either.

She mouths, "I'm all right." I tilt my head and she adds, "I promise," with a brighter smile that reaches her eyes. My heart squeezes in my chest. I haven't had a single moment alone with her yet. She was already sitting with Dom and Caleb when I came into the kitchen with Devin. I didn't get to say a damn word to her before Veronica arrived.

"As soon as we're done, you can have some alone time, all right?" Devin whispers, tickling my ear.

Staring straight into his stunning silver gaze, I tell him, "I swear to God I'll kill you if you can read my mind."

His low chuckle makes me smile. It doesn't go unnoticed that the three members of the Authority watch every interaction like hawks.

There are three dark gray sofas in the room. One long, high-back sofa serves as a focal point, facing a large brick fireplace on the back wall. The other two are smaller and on either side of the first, loosely forming a U. Remy sets up a camera and microphone in front of the fireplace and positions them toward the large sofa.

"This is already going better than expected," Remy comments offhandedly as he does.

"Have a seat." Alec motions toward the longer sofa and I sit close to the middle while catching Lizzie's eyes so she knows to sit next to me. She follows my lead and takes my hand in a firm grasp as she gets comfortable. Devin sits to my left and places a firm hand on my thigh.

"Maybe it's best if only one of you accompanies your mate. Perhaps Caleb?" Natalia purrs as Caleb and Dom both prepare to sit next to Lizzie. The two of them share a look for a moment and then Dom nods, giving Lizzie a small kiss before stalking to a smaller sofa.

"Your statements will need to be genuine. You cannot mention anything about being mates." Lizzie nods as Alec gives his instructions.

"What exactly can we and can't we—" I start to ask, but the bitch in the corner interrupts me.

"Do you think you could control your mate, Devin?" Natalia asks with a devilish smirk.

"He doesn't need to control me," I practically snarl.

"She'll be fine." His large hand finds mine, but I refuse to take it. I didn't ask for this. It's not right and perhaps I am bitter I've been lied to my entire life before being plucked from my existence and thrown into a world with entirely new rules. Even worse, I'm given no grace in that fact.

"I don't believe it." The vampire turns away dismissively and faces Remy. "She's going to ruin everything. It can't be live."

Remy responds as though we aren't in the room. "We should just give them back; it's not worth the risk."

"There's no risk. Grace will follow my lead."

"I don't believe you. It's obvious you have no control over her." Remy dips his chin toward Devin's hand on my thigh and adds, "She can't even follow simple commands."

"I listen to my mate." My nostrils flare slightly as I try to get a grip on my composure. I hate that this prick is getting to me.

"I want to see you bow to him then." A smug smile crosses his face and I have an intense urge to smack it off.

"My mate is only concerned with what pleases me." Power and anger radiate from Devin. Remy noticeably cowers and Natalia narrows her eyes at him, obviously displeased by his reaction to my mate's harsh tone.

Devin's dominance suffocates the room and it's a heady feeling. Devin's silver eyes pierce mine. His aggravation lingers in his words, but I know it's not intended for me. "Do you think it would please me to have you bow to me simply because *he*," he sneers the word, "wants you to?"

Pride flows through me as I relax my shoulders and lean into him to stare into his gaze. "I think it would please you if I sucked your dick in front of them." I purr with a flirtatious smile as my hand gently strokes his inner thigh. I must still be in heat because the idea turns me on. I hadn't intended for the comment to be taken seriously, but as I picture myself on my knees between his legs, taking his cock into my mouth in front of everyone to see, a warmth flutters in my lower belly. So much so that I almost drop to my knees in front of him. My aching core clenches in need as I lick my lips.

"These are the mates that gave you so much trouble? A broken wolf and a bitch in heat?" Natalia's words break the haze of lust clouding my judgment. Alec looks between his two companions with obvious revulsion.

Dom snarls and Caleb's smile slips as he glares at Natalia.

"Enough!" Alec reprimands his colleagues.

My heart hurts for Lizzie. *Broken wolf.* She blows off the comment with the joyful laugh she's known for, all while shrugging and rolling her eyes. I know it hurts her, though. I can see it in her expression.

"Carol will be here in five. Then we'll get this press conference done and over with." Alec walks to the window to study the forest with a stern look on his face. I don't understand how he's aligned with the two of these pricks. I'm also not sure who he is. Or *what* he is.

"I see you have a new pet, Veronica." Remy's eyes travel along Veronica's body with obvious desire. It surprises me since I figured he was *with* Natalia. Even more unexpected is Natalia's heated gaze at his comment.

"I'm her mate." Vince's strong voice is relaxed. He's not threatened in the least. The lack of offense seems to take the wind out of Remy's sails.

"You let the dogs speak for you now?" Natalia picks up where Remy left off. *What a fucking bitch!* All eyes turn to Veronica for her response. She tilts her chin up slightly and leans into Vince's embrace, which makes him smile. She kisses his cheek and then turns to face me.

"Don't mind the bitch in heat comment," she says and I meet Veronica's dark eyes. "You can't help the heat, and there's nothing wrong with being a bitch." She turns in Vince's arms and starts to lead him toward the hall.

"You're turning your back on the Authority, sweetheart?" Natalia casually calls out with a cocked brow.

Veronica offers up the same threatening smirk in return and answers easily. "My back, no, but I've been known to turn a blind eye. Wouldn't you agree, darling?" The older vampire pales and her thin lips press into a hard line.

"Come, pup, this doesn't concern us. You need to show me around." She grins deviously and takes his hand as she waltzes to the doorway. "Start with your bedroom. I have a treat for you."

He flashes her an asymmetric grin and says, "Yes, Mistress." Watching the massive, rugged beast allow his small, feminine mate to lead him away from us makes me smile.

CHAPTER 7

DOM

The sofa groans as I sit back in the seat, but then I immediately lean forward, the nervousness refusing to let go of me. Fuck, I hate that I'm not sitting next to her. Carol bursts through the door in her typical melodramatic fashion. She pops a stick of gum in her mouth and removes her earbuds. The noise flowing from them fills the room. It's a wonder she's not deaf.

Clearing my throat, I attempt to relax but it's next to impossible. The only piece of this situation keeping me steady is that Caleb is right there. Just like I would, he'd give up his life to protect her if anything happened. It offers little relief, though.

Carol smiles brightly as she enters. "So, where are my humans?" Her singsong voice bounces off the walls. She reminds me of Lizzie as she waltzes across the room with confidence. Back before I got ahold of my mate, she had the same carefree air. The thought makes my scowl deepen.

She stands in front of my mate and gasps looking between Caleb and myself. Pointing her finger at the two of us Carol says, "Well, well, congrats to you, lovely lady. A ménage à trois mating; now that's something you don't see every day." Lizzie's cheeks blaze and that faint change in her makes me long for her. To touch her, to run the back of my hand down her cheek and nip the curve of her neck playfully.

Instead, my fingers steeple together in my lap and I sit with this emptiness on my own.

"Fate has certainly blessed you, little human." Her eyebrows raise and she takes one of Lizzie's small hands in both of hers. "Good luck taming these two." Caleb bellows a laugh and Lizzie smiles shyly.

"She's wolf," I say, correcting Carol. "Latent." I say the words with pride; nonetheless Lizzie's smile falls, and she recoils into Caleb. I wish I'd kept my stupid mouth shut. I can't do a damn thing right by her.

"Oh." Carol perks up even more and says, "Well that's wonderful, dear." She purses her lips and taps her heel. "But it's a PR nightmare." My brow creases and Carol answers my unasked question. "A latent wolf on human territory?" She shakes her head. "It'll be called a conspiracy, of course. That we set her up as a spy of sorts." She tsks. "It's a shame, but we're going to have to stay with the human version."

"We're on in five." Alec positions a chair angled toward the sofa and turns the camera on, extending a screen and flipping it so we can view the human newscasters.

"All right, Daddy," Carol answers him easily.

"Daddy?" Grace's curious look almost makes me smile. Devin is going to have his hands full answering our Alpha mate's questions after this morning. She truly has been thrown to the wolves.

"He's not *really* my daddy." Carol winks at Grace and takes a seat, fixing her skirt and tucking a strand of hair behind her ear. She flashes her pearly whites and asks, "No lipstick, right?" She sucks at her teeth while Grace shakes her head, grinning at Carol. A warmth settles through me as I watch Lizzie relax. Carol and Grace are good for her.

Maybe Grace doesn't realize it, but she set the mood the moment we walked in here. Devin's appraising gaze tells me he's aware of it as well. It provides an unexpected comfort.

"She'll be all right." Caleb's words sound in my head as he pats Lizzie's knee and kisses her forehead. A faint blush appears on her cheeks. I love the look of her flushed skin.

"Okay, ladies and gents, I'll field the questions. You just play along." Caleb and Devin nod slightly as Lizzie fidgets with her fingers until Grace takes her hand and squeezes.

"Any questions? It's now or never." Grace shakes her head and Lizzie follows suit.

It seems just then that Grace looks down at her outfit and realizes she's going on camera in sweatpants and a simple gray T-shirt. Lizzie is just as casual in worn, faded jeans and a blush tank top. Both of their faces fresh, without an ounce of makeup on.

From one event to the next, they're thrown into it with no warning. Grace's unease comes and goes quickly as she squares her shoulders. I don't miss Devin's hand squeezing hers either.

Alec hands Carol a mic that she immediately turns on and taps lightly. The sound vibrates through the room, making her smile. There's an innocence in Carol that hundreds of decades of violence have yet to break.

"There's a five-second delay in case we need to cut the feed." Alec speaks only to Carol as he gets behind the camera. "We're live in three, two ..." He finishes by mouthing *one*.

"Hello, Carol." We hear a woman's voice from the screen.

"Hi, Amber. How are you this evening?" Carol's sweet voice takes on an edge of professionalism. It's her mask for the humans. Far less theatrical. She's the Authority's PR dream.

"We're all a bit anxious over here to see the state of Elizabeth Weatherly and Grace Windom. I can see they're sitting with you now. Is that right?" The news anchor's dress shirt remains stiff when she leans in slightly, as if she could get a better view. Her anxiousness is more than obvious and the back of my neck heats with a tingle.

"They are. I can assure you that I was just as anxious watching the offering of Shadow Falls as it aired on the news and saw the clips that were shared on social media. The Authority was prepared to take action and mete out justice had the werewolves of Shadow Falls violated the law. We will always honor our pact with the human nation. However, we have no desire to interfere in this case. As you can see, both humans are doing well. The Authority's investigation has determined that no laws were broken."

"Carol, I have to ask. Why is it that there was such a difference at this offering? We're given so little information that the sight of the Shadow Falls incident was very disturbing for the human population." The anchor drops her tone, matching the somber expression on her face when she adds, "It reminded us all of much darker times."

"As we promised years ago when we formed our alliance, we will not allow supernatural beings to harm humans that reside in areas of treaties." Carol answers with an air of authority and confidence. "Unfortunately, this offering was different due to the mistraining of a wolf. The werewolf collecting Elizabeth Weatherly was given poor advice on how to handle humans. As you can imagine, a paranormal being's touch can be intimidating and forceful." Carol turns in her seat to face Lizzie and tells her, "I can only imagine how scared you were." Her eyes and tone turn sympathetic. "Would you like to tell us how you were feeling during the offering?"

A chill spreads through me and I swear my heart stops. The gulp of Lizzie's swallow is audible.

Lizzie's arms wrap around her midsection as she answers, nodding her head. "I wasn't so much scared as I was shocked when he grabbed me. I wasn't expecting it and then ... Without knowing what would happen, I reacted without thinking." Her voice is small but firm. She tacks on an apology. "I'm sorry." The shock I feel in this moment is genuine.

It takes everything in me not to comfort her, not to tell her she has no reason to be sorry.

"Stay still." Devin's command comes with a force that bows my head. Gritting my teeth, I shut down every emotion. *"We're live,"* he reminds me.

"And how were you feeling, Miss Windom?"

The attention moves to Grace, all of our eyes on her. "I was startled and genuinely scared for Lizzie. She's been my friend for as long as I can remember. She obviously wasn't okay." Grace's eyes find Lizzie's and she squeezes her hand. "My reaction was purely one of trying to help a friend."

"How are the two of you feeling today? Now that you've had time to adjust."

Lizzie and Grace both smile sweetly into the camera. "Oh, much better," Grace answers with a hint of comedic flare that seems to resonate with the anchor. Her lips turn up slightly.

"We're much better today." Grace answers for them both.

"I can't tell you two enough how much the nation is relieved to see that you're happy and well." Carol faces the camera again. "Do you have any more questions for us, Amber?"

The woman on the screen doesn't hesitate to ask, her words rushed, "What is the purpose of the offering? For what reason were they taken?"

Carol's smile slips and she turns solemn. "Unfortunately, I'm unable to divulge that information at this time." I cross my arms and lean farther back in my seat. That's the Authority's game. Keep us separated and divided with a lack of information. "I know that you're aware of those limitations, Amber. Any final questions?"

"Are we going to see these two young women again? Can we be updated on their status?" The newscaster sounds hopeful.

A moment passes, a beat in which Carol doesn't immediately respond, providing me with the thought that someone in this room is speaking to Carol silently.

"That's a possibility, Amber." My eyes flash to Carol. That would be a first. She must be lying. "We understand there is unease in the unknown, and we are doing everything we can to dispel your fears of our species." She smiles so sincerely at the camera. She's such a fucking liar.

I watch my mate force a smile for the camera as they wrap up this charade.

"I need one of you for the fucker in the shed." Devin's words sound in my head. Apparently he's over this and already making plans for the soon-to-be-dead shifter. I'd nearly forgotten about him. My hands form fists at the memory of what Vince told us the rival pack had intended to do to my mate.

I nod. *"I'm all yours."*

"You want me to take care of Lizzie on my own?"

My lips turn down even further at Caleb's question. *"I'm sure she'd rather it just be you."*

"Knock it off."

I don't respond. It's obvious she reacts differently to his touch versus mine. *Why wouldn't she?* Caleb doesn't look like the prick who tortured her. I do. I don't know how to make it right. I can't change the past. I'm just grateful she's going to let me claim her.

That simple fact is proof there's no justice in this world. But I will care for her every way I know how until she feels how much I love her, and until she knows she's safe with me in every sense of the word.

After the niceties have finished, the screen turns black with a loud click and the members of the Authority are quick to move about. That prick Remy starts packing up the camera and Devin stands.

"We ask for a moment," Devin speaks and doesn't wait for a response. Instead he gestures for the pack to head back to the kitchen, leaving Carol with an arched brow. Alec acknowledges Devin's request with a nod before moving beside him as the rest of us continue forward.

I walk behind my mate with my hand on the small of her back. When she leans into my touch slightly, I wrap my arm around her waist. She molds her body to mine with a small sigh. And then she looks up. The small smile vanishes and she noticeably withdraws. It takes all of my effort to remain holding her. She'll get used to it. It fucking hurts, like a damn punch to my chest, but both of us will get past this.

Thankfully I'm distracted. I overhear Alec and Devin's conversation.

"I'm sorry, Dev. I hope you know that I was truly hoping you'd found your rightful mate."

Alpha nods and slaps a hand on Alec's shoulder. "I hold no ill will against you, Alec. I understand how it looked."

"I'm pleased we can part on good terms." Alec pauses before adding, "I may need you soon." This catches Devin's attention and he stops in the hallway as the rest of the pack files into the kitchen, while Remy and Natalia remain in the front room. I stay behind to listen in, making sure my presence is known. Devin gives a slight nod and I get comfortable, leaning against the wall with my arms crossed over my chest. As I listen, I watch Caleb lead Lizzie down the hall to our new room. Jealousy races through me as she takes his hand easily.

"Have you heard about the attacks?"

Devin inclines his head slightly, keeping his expression emotionless.

"The vampires are not faring well now that we're limiting their food supply."

"Then lift the law. It seems simple enough." I agree with Devin. It was a stupid law to begin with.

"Unfortunately, the Authority disagrees. The majority are against it. They don't see a need to drink from a vein when there are other options available. Especially when taking blood from an untested source is the number one cause of sickness in the vampire population."

"Veronica mentioned her coven wanting some changes made to the way the blood banks are run in Shadow Falls."

"Did she now?" Alec's tone holds a curiosity that hints at something I can't quite place.

"She made it clear that the humans wouldn't be privy to any information regarding vampires." Devin's quick to defend Veronica. I nod in agreement again. Not that it's needed. She's Vince's mate and we will support her. Given what happened last night, with the other shifters and their attempt to kidnap Grace and Lizzie, I consider myself personally in her debt.

"That would be paramount."

"Is this the way of it now, donations from humans?"

"Perhaps. But the few that have been running have had disturbing results," Alec confides in Devin and the hairs on the back of my neck stand up.

"How's that?"

"Several vampires have gone missing."

"Surely humans aren't abducting vampires?" Natalia and Remy pause their conversation in the other room as Natalia's wicked eyes drift to Devin and Alec.

"It's not certain what is occurring."

"I see."

"I just hope that if I need to call on you, you'll be at the ready."

"As always, Alec." The two men brace their hands on each other's shoulders. "Next time it would be beneficial for you to come alone." Devin stares at Natalia as he says the last word, startling her. I stifle my grin. Alec chuckles and signals for the two vile beings to leave with him.

It's not until the front door closes that Devin meets me at the threshold of the kitchen.

"Good riddance." I don't hide my disgust for that bitch who called my sweet mate *broken*.

"Agreed. But he had to bring backup in case we had ..." Devin trails off as his eyes find Grace. Clearing his throat, he murmurs so his mate can't hear, "We'll take care of the issue in the shed in just a moment." I remain at my spot on the wall as I watch my Alpha take his mate in his arms. She noticeably relaxes in his embrace the very second he touches her. One day. One day soon, I will have that with my mate.

CHAPTER 8

GRACE

"Dom. You're with me. We have a shifter to question." His tone and the serious expression on every pack member's face keeps the words buried at the back of my throat. I have a million questions and there never seems to be time for Devin to answer them.

His hand lets mine fall and I lace my fingers in front of me, choosing to be silent and wait.

I watch Devin and Dom walk out of the kitchen. His broad shoulders and corded muscles ripple as he stretches out his back and cracks his knuckles.

I have no idea who the hell they're going to "question" but I'm certain they'll be getting whatever information they want out of him. There's a thick tension that can't be denied in the room. Dom's almost as tall as Devin. The sight of the two of them is intimidating. Just watching Devin move with the skill of a predator sends a chill down my spine. But knowing what's underneath that white T-shirt has butterflies fluttering deep and low in longing. I stifle my moan. I am, without a doubt, still in heat.

I hope he isn't long. I notice Lev and Jude smirk at each other before Lev opens his mouth.

"You're drooling a little there." His response makes me huff and with Devin and Dom gone, I'm given a bit of relief. The first bit of it I've felt all day actually.

It's one thing after another, and at that thought, I remember the vampire.

"I'm just a bitch in heat, remember?" I can't help the insecurity from slipping out. In an instant, the two shifters tense.

"She's a bitch and she *wishes* she could go into heat." I smile a little at Jude's flat remark. Patting his hand in thanks as I get up from the kitchen table, I go to search the cabinets. Lizzie's going to need coffee. She's a pain in the ass when she goes through caffeine withdrawal and given everything that's happening, her coffee fix is the last thing on her mind and her mates won't know what hit them. I wish Caleb hadn't taken her the second the interview was over.

I need my friend. I need to know she's truly okay and that

everything will be all right. My throat gets tight, but I simply swallow and busy myself.

"Where's the coffeepot?" I ask as I stand on my tiptoes looking into the upper cabinets searching for some kind of coffee maker.

"We don't have one." I accidently slam the door shut in shock at Jude's words.

"How do you not have a coffee maker?" *Seriously?* They have granite counters and top-of-the-line appliances, but no coffee maker?

"Easy," Lev says, shrugging his shoulders, "we don't drink it."

"Well, that's not going to work. Then you'll really see me be a bitch and Liz will top that. I can guarantee you that." Opening the fridge, I grab the orange juice, but then my nose scrunches and I put the bottle back when I remember Lev drank from it. We're going to have to set up boundaries. I tap my foot while looking through the fridge. Maybe I'll write my name on my groceries. I have to take a deep breath and remind myself that this is my home. My new home. A mix of emotions comes over me and it's hard to keep my composure.

"I need to buy some things I think ..." Instantly, I'm reminded of something I've lost.

"Lev, do you know where my clutch is?"

"Clutch?"

"The little purse I had at the offering." I point to my wrist and shake it as if that'll give him a clue.

His forehead creases. "I don't think he'd like it if you called someone, Grace."

"I just need to run to the store. Whatever store you all go to, I assume it's like any other grocery store?" I question, careful with my words. Lev nods easily enough. Thank God. I need some sort of normalcy.

"Good. I need to get a few things. You can keep my phone. It's not like I'm going to see anyone ever again." The thought makes my heart sink a bit, but I just sigh and shake it off. There are things you can control and things you can't. I learned that a long time ago. There's no use in pining over something I can't have.

"If you want to see someone, Devin will make it happen. You know that, right?"

"No, I don't know that." My words are tight as I whisper. I don't know nearly enough. It feels like I'm falling aimlessly and it's not a feeling I'm used to. There's nothing to grab onto or steady myself with. My gaze drifts to the door. I already miss Devin.

"The Authority likes to monitor interactions between species. But he'd move the world for you. You'd just have to keep it on the down low, you know?" I let his words sink in, but then brush them off.

"It's fine, really," I reassure them both and lean against the counter. I huff a humorless laugh. "Who am I going to call anyway? Shadow Falls is a small town full of asshats." It's still nice to think that Devin would piss off the Authority if I wanted to break their laws.

I give him a small, tight smile. "I don't need my phone; I doubt anyone will miss me anyway." Their eyes turn sad and they need to stop that. "Knock it off. The one person I give a shit about is here with me." I point my finger at them. "And you better believe if she hadn't been Dom and Caleb's mate, then we would've smuggled her here." A smile pulls at my lips. I would beg Devin to move heaven and earth to make that happen if she wasn't here with me.

Reaching back into the fridge, I settle on lemonade. There's only a little missing from the top so, at most, only one set of lips has been on it.

"Anyway, I need my clutch so I can grab some stuff from the store. I don't have much cash, but it's enough." I have almost a grand in savings. "Do you guys use banks?" Jude gives me a sexy grin that makes his clean-cut marine look turn bad boy.

"Which bank do you use?"

"S and N." I tilt my head and frown. "What's so funny?"

"Devin owns that one. And Union Trust." My eyes bulge. *Oh shit.*

"How did you think we make money?"

"I hadn't really thought of that." His words start to sink in as I set the lemonade down. Glancing around the kitchen, it's obvious the pack is wealthy. But ... my mate owns banks? Never in a million years would I think the banks were owned by shifters. "That's odd."

They both grin at me. "How's that odd?" I shrug. I suppose it's not that abnormal, seeing as how the powerful are the ones who control wealth, aren't they? And Devin is quite powerful. "Well, you don't need to worry about money; Devin got you a card to use."

"So what am I supposed to do here?" I fidget uncomfortably before crossing my arms and leaning against the counter. A small voice in my head whispers, *"Be the Alpha's baby maker."* The thought makes me shiver with delight, but at the same time, I long for more.

I barely know him. Yet I feel as if I know him more than anyone. I need far more time to get a grasp on this life before I can even think of bringing another into this world.

"Whatever you want." A stinging sensation travels down my body and my heart slows. *Whatever I want.* It's surreal. Tears prick at my eyes and I don't even know why. Wiping them away, I try to compose myself. What the hell is wrong with me? Lev gets up from the table with a concerned look on his face. "You okay, Grace?"

I nod as he places a hand on my shoulder. "Yeah, I just ... I just don't know what to say." I can do *anything* I want. I sit with those words for a beat. *I can do whatever the hell I want to do.*

I worked so damn hard at too many shit jobs just to escape my dad. I doubt he even cares that I'm gone. I'll never have to work for a lazy asshole again and smile at pricks who come in just to complain to someone. I'll never have to get up at the break of dawn because my irresponsible coworker has a hangover and can't work their shift. I don't have to worry about money. No shuffling payment dates around just so we can make it through the month. My grip tightens on the counter just to stay upright. I never really thought much about any of that. It was just something I had to do. Day in and day out. It was one more thing to survive. Everyone has to do it. And now I don't. I can do anything, yet I have no idea what I should do. I don't even know what I *want* to do. I don't think I've ever dreamed beyond what I could reasonably attain.

Once, Lizzie and I talked about opening our own bookstore; we practically ran the place ourselves anyway. But it wasn't anything that could be a reality. I knew better than to dream for something I'd never have. Hell, I'd just barely been able to escape the shit hand I'd been dealt. I absolutely loved my tiny apartment with Lizzie and making the best with what we had. Other than Lizzie, I had nothing. Nothing worth anything. Thank God I had her.

At least I knew who I was, though. I was the tough bitch with her shit together. I knew life would get better one day and that as long as Lizzie and I were together, we'd survive and make the best of every situation. But who am I now? Devin just bulldozed his way through my life and I don't know what's left in the rubble. I should be grateful; I *am* grateful. But other emotions rage through me. Surprisingly, fear is the overriding one. Am I just supposed to lie down for him and let him knock me up? Which brings me back to my scare this morning. I need birth control.

"I need to get some things." I bite the inside of my cheek, making a mental list. The morning-after pill is listed at the very top. "I know Liz is going to want coffee. Do you have, like, a werewolf coffeehouse?" They grin again.

"You can order whatever you want and have it delivered."

"What if I want to go out and go shopping?" I'm sure as hell not staying here like a prisoner. Even if it is a gilded cage.

"There are a few shopping malls a few towns over. Right now may not be the best time for you to go alone with everything going on."

"What exactly is going on?" All I know is that this morning the werewolves talked to one another silently. And I sat beside Devin with him reassuring me that I would be told everything later.

"It's a bit of a drive but if you want to get out of here, we can take you."

"Way to dodge the question," I retort.

Lev throws his hands up in defeat. "Just name someplace," he suggests and his tone is nearly pleading. "We'll take you."

"What about the nearest coffeehouse?"

With an uncomfortable demeanor, he tells me, "Sorry, Grace, you'll have to order it and have it delivered, but I can take you to one of the malls after?"

I nod. That's not a bad option.

"Let's order Lizzie's coffee and head out so I can pick up some stuff. Which room is hers?"

As I ask the question, Vince strolls into the kitchen wearing sweats, no shirt, and has a belt draped around his neck. The buckle of it hits him in the chest a few times while he walks and a look of irritation crosses his face before he swings it over one shoulder.

"Yo, what're you guys talking about?" He grins mischievously, heading to the fridge.

"Shopping trip." Jude gives a clipped response.

"Ah, I think Veronica said she wanted to go out and get coffee." My lips purse at the mention of Veronica.

"Do you like it when she calls you 'pup?'" I blurt out but the question is riddled with my judgmental tone. Shit. If I could suck the words back in, I would. There's no doubt in my mind the fact she's a vampire has colored my opinion of her. And every detail of what she does. I immediately regret asking, but Vince doesn't take offense. *Thank God.*

"Like it? I love it." He smiles like a proud kid who just won a spelling bee and grabs a soda. Lev snorts a laugh and Jude chuckles.

"Seriously?"

"Yeah. I fucking *love* it when she calls me pup."

"Isn't it like … a little degrading?" I can't help but to ask.

"What's your favorite color?" A broad smile spreads across his face as he leans against the granite counters.

"What?"

"What's your favorite color?" He repeats his question with strained humor.

"Purple."

"Why?"

"Why what?"

"Why is it your favorite color?" A smug look crosses his face.

I nod as I pick up on the point he's making. "There doesn't have to be a reason."

"Exactly." He claps his hands loud in front of him.

"Don't you feel disrespected, though?" His brow furrows and a small frown pulls his lips down. Maybe I pushed too far. Damn my stupid mouth. He finally shakes his head.

"Not at all. I'm earning her pleasure." His smile returns. "And she's earning my trust. Fuck, she has my trust. I know she's going to take care of me." Lev and Jude choke out a laugh again as he tosses the belt back over his shoulder. "Fucking thing keeps getting in my way, though."

"It's just like you and Dev. Isn't it?" Lev asks. My eyes narrow. Fuck no, this isn't like us at all. "He's earning your trust, isn't he?"

"Yeah, but not like that." Vince lets out a bellowing chortle and his silver eyes brighten.

"It works both ways, sweetie. Just because our kink's a bit different from yours doesn't change anything. He's gaining your desire to please him, isn't he? And proving that you can trust him to make sure your every desire and need are met?" I let out a small hum in contemplation.

His words sink in as he strides out of the room, but I end up focusing on a single question.

How can Devin be ensuring my every need and want are met, when I don't even know what I want or need anymore?

CHAPTER 9

LIZZIE

"She called you a broken wolf." The cool air slips against my heated skin at Caleb's words.

He said he would take my pain and turn it into pleasure. We decided together... but this is different. If only I snap my fingers, it all ends. I know that much and hearing him repeat the words, *broken wolf*, has the thought at the forefront of my mind.

I'm naked, on my knees with my head and chest lying on the foot of our bed. I hear Caleb unbuckle his belt and a flood of mixed emotions dries my throat and makes my hands tremble while simultaneously heating my core. "You didn't defend yourself. You hid your emotions and blew it off as though it doesn't matter." He bends down with his mouth at my ear and whispers, "It matters. Don't hide your feelings from me. I'll ask you again and this time there will be consequences if you lie to me. I refuse to let you hide." He straightens his back and runs the leather down my spine, tickling my skin and sending goosebumps down my body. "Tell me how you felt when she called you broken."

My heart races and emotions swarm up my throat.

I don't want to talk about it. I don't want to admit how much pain it caused, how many memories resurfaced ... I don't want to think about it and make it all real again. I lived in happiness for years, avoiding the truth. It doesn't have to be real. I don't have to acknowledge it. Caleb's wrong; it doesn't matter.

"I don't care." I can barely give him my answer. It's the same answer I gave him last time and the time before that. The answer I know will push him to punish me. He'll take care of me after. And I want that. I crave it in a way that drives me to keep this going. I don't know how to explain it. I want this over and over, because in the end, he's going to make it better. He has to. He's my mate.

Smack! I jump as the belt whips through the air and lands hard on my bare thighs, just below my ass. I breathe through clenched teeth, hissing at the pain. Tears cloud my vision. But I'm used to them. Just like I'm used to the pain.

"They called you broken and you don't care?" My head

is so dizzy, it takes me a moment to realize he's waiting for an answer as he rubs the swollen, red marks. His cool touch soothes my heated skin. Caleb's fingers are dangerously close to slipping between my legs. I'd rather he touch me there, but he'd rather whip me. Punish me for not admitting I'm damaged. *Fuck him*. He's not getting that from me. He can beat me until I'm black and blue. Just like all the others. Just like Dom's father. Burying my head into the sheets, I tell myself that's not true. My head thrashes and the splinters of pain deepen. I know all I have to do is tell him it hurts, not the punishing blows, but the fact that I'm broken.

"You care, don't you?" This question is spoken in a softened voice. Staring straight ahead, I don't want to tell him I do, because then what? Is he going to make me face the past?

"No." I brace myself, preparing for the blow that's coming. *Smack*! The belt lands across my ass, making my blood rush violently in my ears.

"Why do you lie to me? Why do you lie to yourself?"

"I'm not lying!" Tears prick my eyes and I let them fall. *Smack*! My skin burns from the repeated strikes of the leather. I find myself pushing against the sweet sting. My pussy clenches in anticipation.

"Stop lying. Tell me how you feel." His tone is tortured. I shake my head as tears fall down my face. Why am I lying again? I can make this stop. I can stop this by just admitting the truth. I shake my head harder. I don't want it to be real.

"She called you broken. How does that make you feel?" I keep refusing to answer. My body trembles as he gently runs the leather across my tender ass. "Answer me!" He's going to belt me again. But I don't want it anymore. I don't want this anymore. My skin is hot and sensitive, each smack bringing me closer to the edge of something else. That's all I want. I want to fall off the edge.

"Caleb," I plead with him.

He lowers his lips to my ear after kissing the crook of my neck and says, "Tell me, tell me."

"Worthless. It makes me feel like a failure." I sob, gasping for air as the pain of my admission flashes through me. It's out. The words flew out of my mouth without my conscious consent. I'm so worthless. A wolf who can't shift. I don't know what's wrong with me. I don't know if I can ever be fixed. "I'm useless. Like I shouldn't be alive." The belt falls to the floor with a loud thud and in an instant Caleb is on me, pulling me up and cradling me in his arms.

"You're none of those things. You're perfect." The words rush out of him and then his lips devour mine. Everything ceases to exist.

I cling to him as he pulls me into his chest and rocks me. There's a sweet sting of pain and pleasure as my ass settles against his thigh. "Look at me." I stare into his silver eyes as he kisses my nose and rests his forehead on mine. He whispers, "You're not broken." My lips part to object. Of course I am. "You were made with perfection. Including your latency." The word makes me flinch. He takes my chin in his hand with a firm grasp. My eyes are caught by his fierce gaze. "You are a latent wolf. And you are fucking perfect." The sincerity and love are undeniable in his admission.

Hot tears prick again and this time I welcome them. His adoration heats my core. Slamming my mouth against his, I push him against the mattress and climb over his hard body. He moans into my mouth. I rock against him and grind into his throbbing erection. My blood heats and races through my body.

I want to thank him for loving me. I'm desperate to please him. Making my way down his body with openmouthed kisses, I nip at his hip bones as he takes out his cock for me. I stroke his thick length as he throws his head back. My lips wrap around the head of his cock and I can barely fit it in my mouth. My teeth scrape lightly against his hardened flesh.

"Open your mouth wider." I do as I'm told, stretching my jaw to accommodate his size. I lick at the bead of precum at the head before bobbing along his length. His hands run through my hair before pushing his length into the back of my throat. I swallow and his girth is almost more than I can comfortably take. My eyes sting and water before he pulls back, allowing me to breathe again.

"Bite me." I look up at him wide eyed. *Bite him?*

"Come on, baby girl ... Bite me." His voice is breathy but still full of authority. He's close to his release. My teeth close around his dick and I bite down, digging into the velvety steel of his flesh.

"Harder." Clamping my mouth shut again, I push my teeth into him. If I bite any harder, I know I'll break skin. I pause, waiting for his next direction. He fists my hair and pulls my head back, causing a small bit of pain. "Bite me like you want to hurt me. Bite me, baby." He's breathing hard and barely able to get the words through his clenched teeth.

It's obvious he's right on the edge. He wants this and I'm failing him. I can give him the pain he needs. He releases me and I seize the chance to sink my teeth into his hard cock. I take half his length into my mouth and bite down as hard as I can. The second my teeth clamp down he shoots his release into the back of my throat and I quickly swallow, moaning around his dick. His head falls back on the mattress as his legs stiffen and tremble with the shock of his orgasm. Once he's no longer pulsing, I pull back and dip my tongue into his slit to get the last drop, making him shiver. My lips curl up into a smug smile as I crawl up his body. *My mate's a freak.*

CHAPTER 10

LIZZIE

I've never felt so sated, so complete, so ... calm and like nothing in the world could ever hurt me. With my front to his back, I can't stop touching Caleb. My arm rests across his hip while my fingers play with the small dimples on his lower back. Caleb runs his fingers down my side, all the way to my thigh before trailing back up although he stares straight ahead. It sends shivers through my body. "How did you feel while I was punishing you, baby girl?"

My eyes pop open and I tense a bit at his question. My ass still stings, yet the reminder of his belt brings on another wave of desire. *As if I could take any more today.*

"It hurt." I answer simply, not wanting to divulge the fact

I wanted the belt to sting across my aching heat.

"Is that all? I thought you may have been angling your ass so I'd hit a certain area." My face flushes beet red and I duck my head into his strong, muscular chest. Caleb laughs low and deep, causing his chest to vibrate. I love the feeling and the sound. "Did you like it?"

"Only a little bit." That's the truth. I wouldn't be afraid of it happening again, but I don't *want* him to whip me. I don't *want* to be punished.

"What part did you like?"

"I don't really know. It's hard to explain. I just know that I wanted it ... across me there ..."

I lean back so he can see my sincerity. "I don't want to be whipped again, though. I don't like it enough to want it again." He nods his head and closes his eyes while he kisses my forehead.

"I understand, baby. I won't do it again unless it's needed." I settle into his chest again while his hands run down my back. "Do you want to try something else? Something for pleasure?" His question piques my interest and I pull back to look at his curious expression.

"Like what?"

"Like a spanking." My cheeks heat and I nod eagerly. Maybe I'm a freak too. Although I should have known that.

Caleb's bright smile makes my chest fill with pride. In this moment I would do anything to please him. He gets on his knees and smacks my ass. Fuck! The sting is immediate and as it wanes, pleasure builds and every nerve ending lights aflame.

He commands, "Up!" I quickly oblige, getting on all fours for him. His hand rubs my ass, grabbing and pulling at the flesh, forcing me to moan. It takes everything in me to hold still for him. "All right, baby. The first few times will sting, but you'll feel it when you get there." His hand comes down hard, causing my body to fly forward as I let out a yelp. I stop myself from falling, fisting the sheets beneath me, and his hand comes down on my shoulder to keep me steady. "Head down, baby." His hand rubs the tender, reddened flesh and then disappears. Bearing down, I hold my breath waiting for the blow. This time it comes down hard on the other cheek. The stinging pain shoots through my body and my eyes water.

"Is it normal to cry?" It doesn't feel right that I want the pain, but can't help the tears.

"Only if you want to. I can go easier on you if you want, baby." I shake my head. No, the heat and the stinging are just right. I need more of it. *Punish me.* As if reading my mind, his hand comes down hard between my cheeks with his fingertips grazing along my pussy.

"Fuck!" My neck arches back and I push my ass higher in the air as he comes down hard again and again and again. The numbing, stinging pain heats my core. My pussy clenches around nothing, the absence making me moan in frustration.

"Good girl." His fingers run through my slick folds and I hear him suck his fingers into his mouth. "You're soaking, baby." He rubs his hands over the sensitized skin. "You want more?"

"Yes," I tell him, moaning out my response. I'm so close, the pleasure building like waves approaching the shore. Slowly but surely, each wave larger than the last. His hand comes down on my upper thighs, causing me to jump. Then he moves back on my left cheek, then the right, followed by my thighs, then finally my aching center. The tears fall easily with each blow. "More," I plead with him, pushing my hot, tender flesh into his hand as he kneads the growing soreness.

"Uh-uh." He pushes two fingers knuckle-deep inside of me and curls his fingers to hit that sweet spot. His thumb rubs my clit while finger fucking me and I know I'm going to unravel on his hand as my body starts to tremble. A hot wave of pleasure rolls through my body as I hear the door open. Turning my head, I see Dom striding forward. I moan his name. His eyes find Caleb's quickly before looking back at me with his brows raised.

"You want to come, little one?" I nod my head vigorously. I'm so close. He watches for a moment while Caleb continues to finger fuck me. Dom's large hand splays against my ass and rubs it gently, soothing the tender skin. I look up at him through my thick lashes and moan at his sweet touch. Caleb removes his hand, leaving me reeling in the immediate loss.

Before I can object, Dom's other hand slides down to my sticky wetness. His fingertips brush along my clit, sending a wave of chills down my spine while simultaneously heating my core. I groan in pleasure into the mattress.

My mates. The pleasure mixes into a concoction of lust to cloud my vision.

I vaguely hear Caleb pick up the belt. He puts the leather against my pussy, trailing the cold, metal buckle along my clit and up to my entrance, while Dom's hands come back to my ass. My eyes shoot open at the feel of his belt. Propping myself up, I turn to look back at Caleb. My heart races. He said he wouldn't unless it was needed. Fear spikes through me. *What did I do wrong?*

"Relax, baby girl. It's not what you think."

Dom massages my shoulders and pushes my upper body back down against the mattress. "I'm going to make you feel so fucking good." My heartbeat picks up and the flood of adrenaline makes the pulsing need between my thighs pound even harder. I trust him to do whatever he wants to my body. He gives me pain I didn't know I needed, and pleasure I didn't know existed.

"Please." It's the only word I can manage. After I speak, Dom's hands move lower, spreading my lips and exposing my throbbing clit. I hear the swing of the leather and then it smacks against my hard nub, sending a jolt of pleasure through my body. There's hardly any force behind the

low, but the feeling is so intense that my body stiffens ar
hakes uncontrollably. Dom holds me in place as a shoc
races through my body, making me cry out in ecstasy. I'
paralyzed with wave after wave of pleasure as Caleb strik
ny clit with the leather again and again, extending m
orgasm. My body shudders in Dom's grasp, overwhelme
vith the mix of pleasure and pain. As the last aftershoc
ubside, I collapse into Dom's arms and he pulls me clos
issing and nipping my neck.

After I come down from the intensity of everything, I fir
nyself between my two mates, held tightly by both of the
nder the covers. I hum my satisfaction into Dom's ches
Mmm, I liked that."

"I don't think I can hit you." His sad eyes tell me he think
e's failing me. That he won't be able to sate me.

"I don't want you to. I just want you to love me." Th
ruthful words are voiced easily. His lips find mine before th
st word is fully spoken, kissing me with passion.

"Isn't she perfect." Caleb's comment is a statement, not
lestion. I would smile, but my lips are being forced open b
om's tongue.

"*She's so goddamned perfect.*" My eyes shoot open a
om's words and my heart pounds. I can hear his mute
ply, yet his mouth is still on mine, his eyes closed i
stasy. Even so, I heard him loud and clear. His eyes sta
osed as he leans his body into mine

as Dom rolls me onto my back and settles between my legs. He pulls back, biting my bottom lip before kissing along my neck and nipping my collarbone. All the while I listen in on their silent conversation.

"I love the marks you leave on her."

"Everyone who sees her will know she's taken."

"I feel like an asshole." Caleb's words are almost a whisper.

"Why?"

"She's not healing because her wolf is hurting, yet I'm enjoying the marks."

"Don't think like that." It's quiet for a moment while Dom lies down beside me, pulling me back into his chest. Caleb kisses my shoulder and spoons me from behind while his hand runs along my tummy. Both of their erections dig into my flesh.

"You smell her heat?" My heat? Oh my God, I'm going to be in heat during the claiming. The thought makes my pussy clench and a small smile plays on my lips, but I bury it in Dom's strong, hard chest.

"Just barely."

"I can't wait to knock her up." My smile widens at Dom's admission. I nuzzle my nose into his chest to hide it as he looks down at me and kisses my hair.

"You think our pups will be latent?" Dom's question shocks me and my smile vanishes. Latent.

"Don't know, I've never met a latent wolf before." His words

are easy, no judgment, no fear.

"She'll love them just as much, won't she?" And with those words, Dom melts my heart. His only concern is how I would react.

"Of course she will. Why wouldn't she?"

"She thinks she's less of a wolf because of it." His words fuel me to push my body into his, wanting as much of him against me as possible. Tears prick again. Fucking tears. I wish I could just stop crying. At least these are happy tears.

"That's all right; she'll learn she's perfect. We'll teach her." The tears stream down my heated face as the realization of how much they love me hits me with a force that makes my body want to bow to them.

Dom's strong hands run along my ass and thighs.

"Do you hurt at all, little one?" His words are clearer and louder now. They were spoken out loud. I don't want him to see that I'm crying so I just shake my head without looking up at him.

"You're lucky I didn't kill your ass." I stifle my laugh at his silent statement.

"I'm a lucky sick fuck. You should've seen how she was dripping from using the belt." There's a pause before he adds, *"It was a punishment, though."*

"What set you off?"

Caleb huffs in the same muted tone as their words. *"Blowing off her emotions like they don't fucking matter. And then she lied to me. I'm not going to let her hide from us. She's denied who she is for too long."*

Dom nods slightly and kisses my hair again.

"Can you hear me?" I think the words as hard as I can. I would concentrate on finding his wolf but I don't know how to.

Lifting my head and searching Dom's eyes, I find nothing but confusion. "Little one, are you all right?"

I look deep into those piercing silver eyes. Why can I hear them, but they can't hear me? As his mouth parts slightly with his brow furrowed in concern, I press my lips to his, gently sucking on his lower lip and pushing my breasts against his strong, hard chest. For the first time, my heart fills with devotion, my hot skin needing his touch.

My wolf can hear my mates. A warm calm runs through me as I feel her against my chest. *My wolf.*

Part III
Broken Heart

CHAPTER 11

DEVIN

Gritting my teeth, I attempt to keep the anger at bay. This is exactly why I left that shit pack. We let him sit for hours, alone and in the pitch black while he came to... but he's still high. "What are you on?" The stupid fucker just grins and lets out an unhinged laugh. The blood on his teeth and his bloodshot eyes make him appear even more deranged.

My wolf presses against my chest, eager to be released. I grimace as the man's foul breath lingers in front of my face. The shifter is bound to the chair in the middle of the shed with silver rope. Trapped and undoubtedly in pain. His left arm is hanging out of the socket. That's going to take a while to heal, but the rest of him is covered in only faint bruises and blood from wounds that have already healed. Dom cracks his knuckles, preparing for another round.

The disadvantage to being shifters is that this could go on forever since we heal so damn fast. I don't have time for this. I need to get back to my mate. My hand flexes as I tilt my head, judging this prick and finding him lacking.

"Fine, I don't really give a fuck anyway." I move back as Dom steps in front of the mangy shifter and takes his anger out on his already fucked-up face. I let him destroy the poor fucker. It's not doing a damn thing, but Dom can't get past the comment from earlier about "the blond one" looking like she'd be fun. A chill runs through my blood remembering what Vince told us about the pack. We've got all the equipment we need in the back of the shed to get answers.

Answers on where they are and how many are left. I had mercy the last time. I won't the next. They'll all die a slow death. Their fate is sealed.

"Did you know Dom's an expert in torture?" I question casually as Dom lands a fist square on the shifter's jaw. Bloody spittle flies out of his mouth onto the ground as his jaw shatters and hangs off his face. "He didn't want to be, but you could say it came with the territory he grew up in." Pain flashes in Dom's eyes and I immediately regret my comment. That was a poor judgment call, but I continue and apologize telepathically. He nods slightly in acknowledgment before continuing to land punch after punch on his victim's face.

The force behind the flurry of blows has the chair that's bolted to the floor shuddering.

I head to the back of the shed and wheel out the IVs and O negative blood. I have to go to the other side to get the key ingredient.

Holding the bag in front of the stupid bastard's face, I tell him, "Liquid silver." I toss the bag back and forth between my hands as my words register on his face. A hint of worry passes through his eyes. Apparently he's not too far gone.

It'll scorch every inch of this bastard's flesh from the inside out. Constantly. No relief will be given as his heart continues to pump the tainted blood throughout his system. "We'll start off with a low dose, just to give you some pain and the motivation to be forthcoming to end the suffering as quickly as possible. You'll be able to answer our questions easily. But if you don't talk, we'll up the concentration until all you can do is scream. We'll let you go for a few hours, maybe a day before we give you some of this." I grab the IV stand. "Fresh blood. Then we'll ask you again. If you don't answer, well ... rinse and repeat."

Kicking the IV stand back, I grab a syringe. I stab the bag in front of him and let him watch the silver flood into the chamber before injecting it into his bloodstream. The fucker immediately screams and thrashes in his restraints. I can practically see the silver flowing in his blood as each part of his body trembles in agony.

"Are you going to talk, or should I give you some more and let you think about it?"

He snarls and grits through his clenched teeth, "Fuck you!"

"Have it your way." I stab the bag again as he writhes violently in a shit effort to get away from me. His pathetic attempt makes me laugh. There's no doubt we have to kill him. The sooner I get the information I need out of him, the better.

"Wait, wait, wait!" he yells as I stick him with the syringe. I leave it there dangling out of his arm as he seethes, staring at the injection site like it's on fire. His breathing is heavy as he scowls, seeming to reconsider.

"Are you ready to talk?" I keep my face expressionless and voice even.

"I'll tell you everything if you let me go." My lips kick up into a smirk and I huff a humorless laugh as I push the plunger down. His screams hardly register as I think about how he may have taken my sweet mate away from me.

My everything. She *is* my life. So his is no longer relevant.

I speak slowly as the silver leaves the barrel, disappearing into his arm. "You'll die after you give me answers. Whether that's right now, in a couple of hours, days, or weeks even, is up to you. I can promise you that I will make sure you are in pain every second that you continue to breathe." His breathing becomes chaotic as he starts to hyperventilate. "Unless you're ready to talk."

"I'll tell you everything," he barely gets out as he writhes in agony.

"Talk." I peer down at him with my arms crossed over my chest.

"Make it stop! Please, I'll do anything!" His eyes plead with me, but I don't give a fuck. I know what they were planning to do to Liz and Grace. He has no sympathy from me.

"Talk." My hard command is repeated without an ounce of emotion.

"It's the vamps. They want the blood bank." His hurried words rush past his cracked lips. "Stop it! Stop it, please!" I keep my expression calm, but his words make my blood pump faster and fists clench harder. I grab the IV and let fresh blood flow through him.

"*Vampires?*" Dom's question fills my head. Our captive won't be able to hear our conversation because he isn't a pack member.

"*I have no fucking idea what he's talking about. They never dealt with vampires when I was a part of the pack.*" I slowly drain the tainted blood into a bucket.

"*Remind me to keep some blood to test. I want to know what the hell they're on.*"

"*Yes, Alpha.*"

The shifter slowly stops shaking as the silver leaves his system. "Talk." Tears fill his eyes at my simple command. "They're going to kill me." He swallows hard, then looks between Dom and me. "They'll kill me if I talk."

"You don't have to worry about that." Crouching in front of him, I tell him, "I'm going to kill you first. I can make it painless and fast. It's up to you." His eyes fall and sobs wrack through his body. "I don't have time to listen to you cry." I grab the bag of silver and pierce it with the syringe.

"No! No!" He tries to back away from me while shrieking, "I'll talk! I'll talk."

"Then talk!" I let my irritation show. I want him to think I'm ready to pump him with silver and leave him in unrelenting agony.

"They want to taint the blood. They're testing different drugs."

"Taint it with what?"

"I don't know. I swear!" His fear is evident as he pisses himself.

"Why?"

"So they can be the only ones. The drug ends their immortality. They'll be the only ones."

"Who is 'they?'" The words leave me in a growl.

"I don't know. We never saw her. She leaves the drugs. All we have to do is get the territory and make the deal with the coven. That's it, man. That's the deal. I swear!" Rage bristles through me. It must be vampires in the Authority.

That explains why they made drinking from the vein illegal. It ensures the others will use the blood banks. This is fucked. My thoughts fly to Veronica and what she knows about all this. She did come on behalf of her coven to make a deal with the pack. I shake my head at the thought. There's no way she could've known. I wonder how eager her rulers are to build the bank. And whether they still drink from the vein.

I'm vaguely aware the fucker in front of me is now silent apart from his pathetic sobs.

"Nothing else? Is that all you have to say?" He shakes his head as his body trembles with the fear of his imminent death. Turning to Dom I ask, "You want the honors?" He nods once as he picks up a crowbar that's hanging on the wall. I walk out, the sound of the shifter's panic ringing in my ears as I close the door behind me.

CHAPTER 12

VERONICA

What is the claiming like? The unspoken question plays on the tip of my tongue as I take a seat in the high-back, black leather chair in the corner of Vince's room.

Yesterday was nothing more than fun. It was the first time in a long time that I've felt alive. Perhaps that could explain why I'm riddled with emotions that pile on top of one another.

"You were right; it ended quickly," Vince states.

Burying down the unwanted emotions, I nod. "It was much better without me there." Taking in the modern furniture that's quite masculine and not at all to my liking, along with his king-sized bed, I comment, "We'll have to add an addition if you expect me to stay here."

There's a darkness of worry that stretches in Vince's gaze. "I can't leave my pack."

"I'm aware, but I can't store my shoes in your closet, so ... addition?" I offer him, again feeling a war brewing inside of me. The air feels lighter even, as if it threatens to dizzy my thoughts. In a quick motion, a flash of a second, I rid myself of my dress.

"We can build on whatever you'd like," Vince agrees easily, his gaze moving to my bra that I quickly undo and toss in his direction.

"You're insatiable," he comments and I ignore it, other than to smirk. I'm not usually, but him ... inwardly I remind myself that vampires are not susceptible to the "heat" of a mate's desire. Yet ... I feel this unyielding pull.

"I'd like you to tell me everything about this pack." In another quick movement, one I'm not certain Vince can even register, I rid myself of my lace garter and panties, leaving myself bared to him. "The coven knows very little ... other than the basics filed with the Authority."

Vince grins back at me. "About *your* pack, you mean."

My grip tightens on the armrest. I am his mate. There's a fluttering in my heart that wasn't there before.

Cocking my brow, I correct myself. "Yes, my big bad wolf." I spread my legs, exposing my cunt to him and with a single finger I motion him to come to me. "Let me come on your tongue first and then you'll tell me everything about *my* pack."

His asymmetric grin does something awful to me. It pulls something from deep within and heats my body from head to toe all at once. As he crawls to me, his hulking shoulders flexing and his silver gaze never leaving mine, I feel more vulnerable now than I can ever remember.

His touch is hot as his hand grips the inside of my calves, spreading my legs wider for his broad shoulders. In between kisses up my leg to my inner thigh he tells me, "I'll get you off."

Kiss. "And then tell you about our pack." Kiss. "Our history." Kiss. "The claiming that will happen tomorrow." Kiss. "And anything else you want to know."

My fingers splay through his hair as my head falls back and his lips find my clit. He sucks gently and then his large hands take possession of my hips, pulling me closer to him. My legs wrap around his shoulders as I lean back, getting lost in his touch.

He pulls back, staring at my slick folds, and whispers, "We only have one night together, and then we have forever."

Forever. My heart stirs in a way it's not meant to at the word. Before it can take command of my thoughts, Vince devours me and delivers me pleasure like I've never felt before.

CHAPTER 13

GRACE

Impatience is my sole companion as I stare at the bedroom door, waiting on Devin. We need to talk. I'm still coming to terms with everything that's happened and I'm sure as hell not ready to be a mother.

Pups? Do I give birth to a wolf? I'm on the verge of a nervous breakdown as I pace the length of Devin's massive bed. My only identity is his mate. That's who I am. He's taken control of everything and left me with only his plans for our future. I feel backed into a corner and yet I keep thinking if only he didn't leave me alone with my thoughts, I'd be fine. I know deep down I can trust him and I'm very aware that I love him with every part of my being. But the idea of submitting and not knowing what his plans are ... it puts me on edge in a way I'm certain changes my life. I don't want to be a baby factory and that seems to be exactly what Devin's plan entails.

It's too much. Too soon.

The door creaks open and I turn stiffly to see Devin. The sight of him causes me to take in a sharp inhale; his shirt is stretched tight across his broad shoulders and it's covered with blood. His stern expression softens as I run to him with concern.

"Devin." I can barely do anything but whisper his name. "Are you—" He takes my hands in his, keeping me from reaching out to him.

"Don't touch, sweetheart." He gives me a small smile, seemingly pleased with my worried expression. The worry is all-consuming. "I'm all right."

"What happened?" I clasp my hands together in front of me to prevent myself from running my hands over his body in search of the wound. All the while my heart races.

"It's not mine." I take a hesitant step back.

"Don't worry. Everything's taken care of," he says, his tone casual as he walks past me to enter the bathroom, stripping down as he goes. I'm left speechless at the door.

I'm stunned only for a moment before anger creeps in.

This is exactly what I'm talking about. I need to know what the hell's going on and Devin doesn't tell me a damn thing. Gritting my teeth, I stalk after him and shove the already cracked door open. It bangs against the wall, which gets Devin's attention as he steps into the shower. *Good.* He glances back and raises his brows, but continues to walk into the stall.

"Why don't you tell me anything?" Tears prick at my eyes and I wish they didn't. It's not fair that I get so damn emotional and he seems completely unaffected.

"Why are you upset?" He motions for me to join him after he lets the spray flow down his hard, tight body. My eyes glance down involuntarily to his thick cock and I close my eyes, wishing this godforsaken heat would leave me. The sight of his naked, wet body makes my core heat. I stifle the moan threatening to rise up my throat.

"You don't play fair," I murmur with my eyes still shut. He gives a low chuckle, and it's followed by the sound of him walking toward me. His large hands gently tug my shirt up and I help him accomplish his task by raising my arms. With a sigh I open my eyes to find a small smile playing at his lips. His silver eyes are full of devotion as he leans down to kiss me chastely. I part my lips and lean into his touch, but he nips my lower lip, causing me to gasp as he pulls back.

"What did I do to upset you?" After a moment of letting his words sink in, I shake off the lustful haze and square my shoulders.

"You don't tell me anything." As the words leave me, I

realize I sound like a petulant child. I wish I could take them back and start over. It seems I've been thinking that far too often recently.

"That's not true. I answer every question you ask." His brow furrows in confusion at my statement.

I stop myself from yelling in an effort to have a civilized, adult conversation. "Then whose blood is on your shirt?"

"You don't need to know that."

Well, fuck the adult conversation. As I step closer to him, I shout, "This is what I'm talking about, Devin."

"If I don't want you to worry about things, then I'm not going to tell you. That's final." His voice is even and full of authority. Power radiates around him, but I ignore it as my heart clenches in denial.

"I can't do this. I can't be in the dark about things and stay shut away pumping out babies for you."

His forehead pinches. "Is this about having my pups? Do you not think I'm a good enough mate? That I won't be a decent father to our children?" His eyes betray the emotionless mask he wears. They're full of pain and doubt.

I second-guess my conviction at his obvious insecurities.

"I never said that, Devin." I try to ease some of his hurt before I realize he's changed subjects. "And that's not what I'm talking about. You don't tell me things unless *you* think I need to know them. Which isn't fair. I know nothing about all this. It's even worse because I was led to believe lies before."

My hands wave chaotically in the air and I huff in frustration. "Why the fuck is there blood on your shirt?"

"Why don't you trust me?" He steps closer to me and I instinctively take a large step back. My back hits the wall, making me jump at the sudden contact. "Are you afraid of me?"

I shake my head and answer evenly and immediately, "You intimidate me, but I know you won't hurt me."

He steps closer and gently lifts my chin to kiss me. His forehead rests on mine as he closes his eyes and whispers, "Never. I'll never hurt you."

"I really don't care for being kept in the dark." His silver eyes open and stare into my own. He seems to be searching for something and I don't know what. "It makes me feel uncertain and like I can't control anything."

He sighs heavily before turning his back to me and getting in the shower again. The water runs down his gorgeous naked body as he says, "I'd prefer for you to trust my judgment, but if you insist ..." He sighs again and catches my eyes roaming his body. I can't help it. He gives me a knowing smirk, which makes me blush. "The blood is from a shifter who came to the offering." His words ground me.

"What kind of shifter?"

"A wolf. From my old pack." I stare at him, willing him to explain. After a moment, frustration grips me as I realize he has no intention of telling me any more info. It's like pulling teeth with him.

"Why was the shifter from your old pack at the offering?" Devin stops shampooing his hair to look at me. His eyes travel down my body and back to meet my gaze. Foamy suds drip in heavy dollops.

"Strip and get in." He steps under the hot stream of water to rinse. My lips purse at his short command, but I obey. Only because I was going to anyway. At least that's how I justify it.

His hands find my hips as soon as I enter and he pulls my body close to his, resting his chin on my shoulder. "They were there to take you and Lizzie. Or at least that's what they decided when they got there." My body stills in fear. A million questions threaten to burst from my lips, but he continues to talk as he reaches for the body wash. "They want their territory back." He lathers the soap and then massages my body, starting at my shoulders. His strong hands feel like heaven and his touch brings a sense of ease that's at odds with what he's telling me. He kneads my tense muscles and I lean into his warm, expert touch. "Apparently they had a deal with some vampires."

"Veronica's coven?" I'm barely able to make the words coherent as a blissful moan takes over my body.

He chuckles at my effort. "No, sweetheart." He kisses my cheek before adding, "I don't think so. I'm not sure who yet." He turns me in his arms and I rest my forearms on his chest. "Have I told you enough?" I look up at him through my thick lashes and try my best to think. His touch is so soothing and comforting that it's hard to remember why I'm angry.

"You were upset that I keep you in the dark. Are you still mad at me?" How does he do that? My brow furrows.

"Are you sure you can't read my mind?" He laughs and leans down to kiss me, which I more than welcome.

"I'm sure. But that doesn't answer my question."

"I'm not mad. But I don't like having to pull information from you. I wish you'd just tell me."

"And I wish you'd trust me. When I say you don't need to worry, I wish you'd believe me and stop pushing me." I step out of his hold, not liking his response, and reach for my conditioner. I coat my hair and step farther away to gather my thoughts.

"It makes me feel weak when I do that." I nod, agreeing with my own words. That's really what it comes down to.

"When you do what? Trust me?" I shake my head.

"When I put all my faith in you and submit to whatever you want." I lean my head back to rinse my hair but maintain eye contact as I tell him, "It makes me feel weak."

"Do you think our pack is weak?" His question catches me off guard.

"Of course not."

"They all submit to me. But you don't think they're weak?"

"That's not the same." I rinse off and step out of the shower.

He follows, but reaches for a towel before me and wraps

it around my small body, pulling me into his hard, wet chest. Our naked bodies touching make me arch my neck, wanting him to kiss, lick, and bite the exposed skin.

"It is the same. They trust my judgment, knowing that what I decide is what's best for everyone. They're each strong and worthy of being Alphas themselves. But they choose to let me lead and have faith that I'll ensure their safety and happiness above all else. Yet you," he says and rubs the towel along my body, drying me off, "you don't have the same faith. And you're my mate." The last sentence is thick with emotion. "When I met Caleb and Dom, I didn't say a word. I kept walking and they followed. They never questioned my authority or judgment. Never. Yet you've consistently questioned me."

"Really?"

"Yes, at every point you seem to enjoy fighting with me."

"No," I say and let out a small laugh. "I don't *enjoy* fighting with you. I was asking about Caleb and Dom. I don't understand why they would just follow."

He hesitates, searching my eyes again. "Come, I'll tell you more. Maybe hearing how easy it was for the others will help you." I doubt that, but I'm eager to hear any information he's willing to share with me.

"Can you tell me about your old pack too?"

"What do you want to know?"

"Everything." I want to know *everything*. I feel like I'm the only one who's clueless and I'm tired of it.

"Okay. Well, for starters, I hate my old pack and they are worthy of my contempt." I crawl on the bed and wait for him to sit. Patting the spot next to me, he side-eyes me before lying on the bed. With his arm wrapping around me, he pulls me in and I don't object to his touch in the least. Even if it is distracting. "My father was Alpha." His hand runs through my damp hair as he talks. "I was a pup when he died and I hardly remember anything about him. I know a little of my mom, but when he died, things changed quickly and got out of hand so suddenly." His hand stills as he takes a deep breath.

"I was too young to take over; it was my right, but I was only about ten or so. No one fought for the position. A shifter by the name of Sarin took over and started changing things." His brow furrows and he stares straight ahead as he continues. "The pack started dealing drugs. My mother became addicted. I remember more of her than my father. I know I loved her. I did. But I was angry with her. It felt like she may as well have died with my father the way she ignored us." His fingers pinch the bridge of his nose and he heaves in a deep breath. "She died a year or two later and that's when things got worse."

I rub his chest in encouragement. Placing small kisses on his shoulder, I tell him, "I'm so sorry, baby." He kisses my hair, acknowledging my words.

"One day, the day I left, I heard them at the fighting

ring." He swallows before adding, "They used to make money by betting on the fights and taping them to sell on the black market." A chill goes through my body. Suddenly, I don't know if I want him to continue. "I heard Lev. He was crying. They threw him in with two wolves. Not shifters, just animals. Starved and angry animals."

"Oh my God." I let out a gasp as tears prick my eyes.

"I knew he'd heal, but only if he could fight them off. I was able to get him out and run before they killed him. No one stopped us." He finally meets my eyes. "Did you notice the scar on his nose?"

I nod and whisper my admission. "I thought he broke it."

"It's scarred from the wolves. I didn't realize the bones had to be placed together to heal right. I've offered many times to break it," he says and chuckles, lightening the mood. "But he wanted to keep it. To remember." His hand gently tucks a loose strand of hair behind my ear. "He may joke and smile, but he's still hurting. They would've let him die. All for entertainment and a bit of money." I bury my head into his shoulder, wiping my stray tears on his warm body.

The urge to cry nearly overwhelms me but I fight back the tears, eager for Devin to continue. Pressing my skin against his, I nestle as close as I can and wait for him to continue.

With a deep breath, he does.

"We left that night and I was determined to start a new pack. I wouldn't ever go back. By then I was fourteen and just coming into adulthood. We met Vince first, only a few days after leaving. He was out hunting in wolf form, alone after his parents died. A bear had ventured into their den at night. It was just the three of them. His dad eventually killed the bear, but his wounds were too deep and he bled out before he was able to heal." I swallow hard and try to get rid of the knot in my throat. I hadn't expected all this heavy information.

Each one of them damaged in a way I could never know.

"Vince was hurting and in deep need of comfort and companionship. He was a bit older, but when I led us toward the river, he followed. A few weeks later, we found Dom and Caleb. They were fishing, two rogue wolves who'd fled their shit pack together. I found out eventually that Dom had killed his father and uncle, then taken Caleb with him before the rest of the pack went looking for them. When we saw them, I said nothing. I simply acknowledged their presence and continued to lead my small pack south, to warmer lands before the winter storms would cause us too many problems. They followed us. At first they kept a few miles behind. But one night when we set up camp, they came and sat around the firepit as though they belonged." He smiles down at me before lying on his side and trailing his fingers down the curve of my hip. "And they did belong. I knew they'd come so I'd cooked extra meat and left it to the side for them. For whenever they decided that they could trust us."

"I love hearing all of this. Don't stop." He chuckles at my

soft words and kisses the tip of my nose.

"Jude was more difficult. He's more reserved. We noticed him while we were hunting down south. Like Caleb and Dom, he followed. But he stayed in wolf form and didn't approach us for nearly a week. A few times I thought he'd changed his mind and decided we weren't the right pack for him."

"Why?"

"I'm not sure. I never asked and he hasn't offered his thoughts. It's not my place to question his hesitation." My lips part to object, but then I decide to keep quiet and let him continue.

"When he did finally confront us, he came to me in human form and asked who we were. I told him and offered him a place in our small pack. We were all just barely men, but we were a strong pack at that point. He nodded and asked, 'When will you be taking your home back?'" Devin lets out a heavy sigh. "I looked at my small pack and knew it was enough. I decided that day to turn around and take my home back. Well, I burned it to the ground actually. It was too easy to take over. Most of the children were dead or sold. Half the pack was unconscious or strung out from whatever drug they'd taken. I challenged the Alpha, but the coward ran. We torched everything to the ground and started over." A somber expression takes over. "When the Authority heard, they came and agreed that I had the right to challenge for the territory. I was young and naïve to think there wouldn't be consequences. Thankfully, they were less interested in the laws I'd broken and more interested in discussing other terms. Alec helped us financially until I got my footing in stocks and a few startups. For years, making our pack a stable home was my only objective, until we had far more than enough. And then I started dreaming of you. I started living for the day that I'd meet you."

My heart clenches at his words as his strong hand tilts my chin up and he leans down to softly kiss my neck. "I want sons and daughters, Grace. I want a family. A strong, healthy family." His silver eyes find mine. "I understand that you're young and haven't fantasized of this like I have. But it's all I want." The bed groans beneath us as he gets onto his knees and trails warm kisses down my body to my stomach. "I would trade it all just to see you swollen with my pups." He kisses just below my belly button and the sight makes my body heat. I can see him holding me, rubbing along my body as he listens to our unborn child growing inside of me.

"I—" I don't know what to say. I speak without thinking, "I want that too. I do. But not yet. I don't think I can be a mother yet." My voice pleads with him for understanding. He closes his eyes and kisses my stomach sweetly.

"I understand." He nods his head and lies next to me again, rubbing soothing circles on my back. "I do, sweetheart. And it's all right. In fact, it may be for the best that we wait. I may have to leave soon. I need to talk to the Authority about this new development."

"What does that mean? I don't understand." I'm overwhelmed with concern. "Leave for how long?"

"I'm not sure yet, sweetheart." He rests his forehead on mine and smiles. "But as soon as I know, I will tell you. I promise." I can't help the pleased smile that grows on my face. *Progress.*

"Thank you." I breathe out the words before finding his lips with mine and pushing my body against his. He chuckles at my lack of subtlety.

"You'll be too sore for the claiming tomorrow." I shake my head, but refuse to leave his touch. Nipping his top lip, I rub my thigh over his hip. He groans as my heat rubs against him. "Once more." He breaks away and waits for me to meet his gaze. "But then you'll have to wait. I don't want you to be hurting."

"It'll be a good hurt." I rub my cheek against his chest. He laughs again and rolls me onto my back, caging me in with his strong, hard body.

"One more time, sweetheart." My head falls back against the mattress in incomparable ecstasy as my mate makes love to me, with long, gentle strokes until we peak together, finding our release in each other's arms.

CHAPTER 14

LIZZIE

"Baby girl, wake up." Caleb's words barely register as I groan in displeasure. I was having such a wonderful dream, but for the life of me, I can't keep a grasp on it and it leaves me without permission. I push against his hard chest.

"Five more minutes." Both he and Dom huff a masculine laugh at my reluctance to wake up.

"Wake up, little one. Do you feel your wolf?" My eyes shoot open at the mention of my wolf. She came to me. I *felt* her.

"You healed while you were asleep."

"All my hard-earned marks are gone." Caleb pouts playfully, but I can see the overwhelming happiness in his eyes.

With disbelief, I quickly throw aside the bit of blanket remaining on my body and turn to look at my ass and thighs. Tears prick my eyes when I see that she healed me. *My wolf.* She came back to me. I close my eyes and try to feel her, try to talk to her, but I feel empty and alone. My lips pull down and a sadness flows through me. I don't want to hope that she'll come back. I can't take the disappointment.

"Hey, don't be upset." Caleb tugs my bottom lip with his teeth and kisses me.

"Do you think she can hear us?" I nearly react to Dom's unspoken words. The muted voices in my head ask, *"Can you hear us, little one?"*

"Can you hear me, baby?"

Keeping my eyes shut, I will them to hear me, admitting the words I'm afraid to say aloud. *"I love you. I love you both so much."*

"Give us a sign if you can hear us." I hear Dom's voice and those damn tears threaten again.

"I can hear you!" I nearly yell in my head. *"I love you! Listen to me!"*

"Are you all right, baby?" Caleb asks out loud and tears form in my eyes. They still can't hear me. I shake my head and let the tears fall as I sob in his arms.

"It's all right; it's a good sign." I try to speak, but give up when I realize it's no use. For so long I thought she'd left me. I thought she'd died. And now she came back, but left me again. She didn't give me a chance to heal her.

"We need to talk to her about the ceremony." Dom's voice echoes in my head and I do my best to settle down. Caleb's right. It's a good thing. It's a good sign that she came out at all. Shaking out my hands, I take in deep, steadying breaths before brushing my tears away.

"Baby, we need to talk about how you want us to claim you tonight." My eyes open at Caleb's words.

"What do you mean?"

"Well, there are two of us so we're not quite sure how we're going to handle each other. We don't want to be rough with you or fight over you." He runs a hand through his thick hair and looks past me at Dom before continuing. "When the moon is at its peak, we may be difficult to deal with. It brings out our wolves and our primitive side." He glances at Dom again and opens his mouth, but closes it.

Dom places a gentle kiss on my shoulder and says, "We weren't sure if you wanted us to take you like that for our first time."

"Oh." Surprised but also intrigued, a rush of arousal dampens my core. The thought of them sharing me, taking turns giving me pleasure and taking theirs from my body, makes my entire being heat with anticipation. Licking my lips, I arch my head to look at Dom over my shoulder. His eyes are drawn to my exposed neck before he meets my blue-eyed stare. "Were you thinking it would be better to ..." I say and hesitate. *Fuck me* doesn't sound appropriate to use when referring to me giving them my virginity. I don't have to finish my question, though.

He swallows, holding my gaze. "We may be gentler."

"The sooner, the better. Your heat is coming on strong now. It's fucking killing me to wait." My lips curl up into a smile at Caleb's impatience. I glance between my two mates.

"How?" They share a look before Dom answers.

"We want to break your hymen together." My eyes widen with disbelief. Both of them? Together? "No, no. Sorry." He chuckles, looking down at the bed before looking back at me. "With our fingers." His smile broadens at my obvious relief. "We don't want to hurt you. And I think we can all agree that, for your first time, that may be a bit much." The words *for your first time* linger in my head as I stare back at my beast of a mate. My body heats and cools at the same time as I remember him stroking his huge cock over my stomach. I lick my lips again with anticipation.

"Do you want to do it now?" My teeth sink into my lower lip. I'd be lying if I said I wasn't nervous. "It's going to hurt, isn't it?"

"Only for a little bit." Caleb gets on his knees and leans down to the crook of my neck. "We won't leave you in pain, baby girl."

"We'll take care you."

I nod and settle on my back between my mates. Looking

between my savage beast and skilled hunter, both of them hold expressions of longing and desire. I run my hands along their chiseled abs and watch as Dom shivers and Caleb leans in for more of my touch. I bend my knees and part my legs for them as another wave of heat flows down my body, pooling in my core, causing my clit to throb. Caleb's fingers travel down my tummy, leaving goosebumps in his wake. He gently presses on my clit, rubbing small circles on the sensitive nub.

My nipples harden instantly as my head falls back in pleasure.

"It'll only hurt for a minute. Dom will take you first and then me. Okay, baby?"

I nod with my eyes closed as numbing tingles flow from my core to my limbs, making my body stiffen with the need for release. He dips two fingers inside of me and the slight stretch is welcomed. My pussy clamps down on his fingers, needing more of his movement to get me off. Dom joins with two fingers and the added girth stretches me to a point of slight pain. My mouth drops open, forming an O as the sensation leaves me feeling full already. Wincing, I wiggle involuntarily as I relax around their shallow movements. They slowly finger fuck me, moving together and putting pressure on the sweet, rough spot on my front wall. The pain quickly subsides. I arch my back and moan as my skin heats and my toes go numb. My heels dig into the mattress as I push myself into their hands.

Dom's other hand moves to my clit and he rubs my own arousal against the throbbing nub in strong, unrelenting circles. I buck against the overwhelming sensation. "Yes!" *Fuck, yes!* Caleb's free hand holds my hip down as they finger fuck me harder, no longer in unison as my need to cum has me thrashing against their hold. The building waves threaten to overwhelm me. It's then that I feel a pinch of pain, followed by the enormous weight of pleasure coursing through my body. The waves crash against me as Caleb kisses my shoulders and Dom moves between my legs.

There's a slow, stinging pain as he pushes his thick cock inside of me, stretching my walls. *Thump, thump,* my heart hammers. It's happening. I'm giving myself to my mate. My heels dig into the mattress as my eyes close and I try to relax around his enormous size. I'm so full and so hot; the heat is nearly unbearable. With my chest rising and falling, my breathing comes in chaotically. He pulls out slowly, not all the way. At first there's relief, but my body immediately misses his touch. He rocks into my body, pushing more of himself into my aching core. His head falls onto my shoulder as he groans, "You feel so fucking good." He leaves an openmouthed kiss on my collarbone before slowly sliding in and out of me again. The heated sensation pulsing through my sensitized body makes me moan.

"You're doing so good, baby." My head lazily rolls to the side so my hooded eyes can focus on Caleb and the sweet kisses he's leaving down my shoulder and on my breasts. He sucks a nipple into his mouth while pinching and kneading the other. Dom's fingers pinch and circle my swollen clit. My two mates work together to overwhelm my senses with undeniable pleasure. My body bucks off the mattress as Dom pushes inside all the way to the hilt and stills. My walls pulse around his cock and arousal leaks down my thighs as I come violently and unexpectedly, trembling beneath their touch. The sensation is paralyzing. Dom's hips push against mine as he thrusts into my aching heat, prolonging my release. A strangled cry leaves me in pleasure as he picks up his pace. His massive frame hovers over mine before he reaches around me and lifts my small body off the bed. His large hand grips the nape of my neck, helping him to fuck me with ease. Each forceful pump of his hips sends my body into a heated shock. White lights dance in my vision and my voice is stolen as I silently scream my pleasure.

He pulls me to his chest as he lies down on his back. His strokes slow as Caleb approaches behind me. My numb body sparks to life as Dom stills deep inside me and Caleb presses the head of his dick into my ass. I push off of Dom's chest, but he holds me still. "Shhh, push against him. It will help." I whimper at the foreign sensation, but do as Dom tells me. As Caleb slowly pushes himself into me, the slick but cold lubrication from his arousal quickly heating, I feel overly stretched and full. And hot. So damn hot and full.

I shake my head on Dom's chest and tell him, "Too much."

Caleb pauses and then kisses my shoulder. "Try again?" he questions and I can only nod, my head laying weakly against Dom's chest. I want them both. At the same time. Even if it is too much.

He's gentle and slow, encouraging me to take all of him. All the while, Dom nips and kisses every inch of my skin he has access to.

He holds my hips steady and kisses me with a tenderness that soothes my nerves. My body shakes and a cold sweat covers my body as they move, first Dom and then Caleb, in and out of my body. I tremble as another wave of heated numbness overtakes my body, starting at my toes and building in the pit of my stomach. Caleb's fingers rub my clit and his other hand pinches and pulls roughly at my nipples. Their pace speeds up as I pulse and come brutally from their unrelenting touch. My hands fist in the sheets, my body tensing.

Wave after wave of intense pleasure hits me, each greater than the last as they continue to use my body, claiming it as theirs, thrusting ruthlessly, taking their pleasure from me. It feels like an endless orgasm shocking my numb body over and over again. Time loses all meaning as my orgasms flow together. At last they finally find their release, each buried to the hilt inside of me. I drift off as they each kiss me, their touch warm on my lips, my neck and my shoulders, whispering soft words of love and devotion.

CHAPTER 15

GRACE

I can't help but to compliment her. "Your car is really nice."

In reality, I fucking *love* Veronica's car. It's an Aston Martin. *Holy shit, I'm riding in an Aston Martin.* I'm freaking the hell out! But not on the surface. Nope. Staying cool and calm and collected. Even though she can probably hear my heart racing with excitement.

"I fucking love your car!" Lizzie offers no pretense, bursting at the seams with excitement. It's the first time I've seen her genuinely smile since we got here. Her schoolgirl level of enthusiasm makes my lips kick up into a grin. It's contagious. The two of us are in the back with Vince riding shotgun. And of course Veronica's driving. My fingers run along the expensive leather and I take in every little detail.

She's loaded. Is every shifter dripping in wealth?

Her gaze meets mine in the rearview.

"It's pretty fucking awesome." I cave. At least I'm not drooling.

Veronica gives us a small, knowing smirk and says, "It's a guilty pleasure." Her eyebrows raise as Lizzie sucks on her drink. "Don't you dare spill that in my car."

Lizzie shrinks back slightly but doesn't lose her smile. "I won't, *Veronica*." She drawls out her name and adds, "Can I call you V?"

"V?" The smooth skin on her forehead pinches.

"Yeah. V for vampire and Veronica." Lizzie's simple explanation has Veronica grinning broadly with those damn fangs on full display. I suppress my shiver and keep telling myself it's just fine she's a vampire. As Devin insisted this morning, she's part of our pack now.

"Call me whatever you want, little wolf." She slaps at Vince's hand as he tries to change the station on the radio. Her admonishment earns her a wolfish grin from her mate.

Lizzie starts mouthing the words to the song before going back to her favorite pastime: sucking down her iced coffee. I desperately need to talk to her in private, but I just can't wait any longer.

"You seem happier now than you were earlier." She takes another sip and nods.

"I'm feeling a lot better." She looks toward the front seat at Vince before making eye contact again. "It's just a lot to happen at once." Her words are soft, but the twinkle in her eyes is still present.

"So you're a werewolf?" It's odd that I still think of her as the same Lizzie. My bubbly partner in crime, yet there's a side of her I didn't know existed.

"Sort of." She twists the hem of her shirt between her fingers. She keeps her voice low, and thankfully Vince and Veronica don't pry although I'm sure they can hear. "I've never shifted or been a part of a pack that I can remember." She breathes in deep while her lips pull down. "What I do remember I'd rather forget."

"I can't believe you never told me." I take her hand in mine.

She shakes her head and squeezes my hand tight. "I never would have. I've never thought of myself as a wolf." She squirms uncomfortably in her seat and glances at Vince again before adding, "I felt her, though." Her eyes light up and she holds back her smile. "It's been years, way before I met you. But she's back."

"How do you feel her?" It's shocking; exhilarating. All of it is overwhelming and I can't help but to want more. "I want to understand."

"I just can. It was only for a second and then she vanished. I don't know how to control her." She sucks the straw back into her mouth.

"That's good that your wolf is coming back, Lizzie," Vince states simply and nods. Then he smirks and teasingly adds, "She must've found something she liked." Veronica smacks Vince on the chest. "What?" he asks in that voice a kid uses when they've been caught stealing cookies.

"You know what." Her eyes find mine in the rearview. "So, where are we going first?"

"Pharmacy, please?"

"You got it, Alpha." I blush at her comment. My eyes dart to Vince to see his response, but he doesn't give anything away. His hand brushes along Veronica's thigh as he lifts up her skirt.

She gives him a side-eye. "What the hell do you think you're doing?"

"I want to see if you've still got that garter on."

"I took it off. No panties either this go-around."

His eyes bulge. "In this scrap of a skirt!" She smiles at his outburst and the tip of her tongue plays with her fangs.

"You're too easy, pup."

"So you *are* wearing something?"

"Hmm," she hums noncommittally.

"Is that a yes?"

"Hmm." He frowns at her response, but his eyes hold nothing but desire.

Finally he settles on, "That's fine." Veronica's lips curl upward in a pure female expression of triumph. He relaxes back into his seat. "I have ways of finding out." He turns to look back at the two of us. "So, *ladies*, how's everything going?" Lizzie blushes slightly at his question, which makes that wolfish grin return. "Are you ready to be claimed?" Veronica stiffens a little, but Vince doesn't seem to notice. I notice, though.

"I want to get something pretty to wear." His brows raise and he chuckles.

"You know you won't be in it for long … and it'll probably get destroyed." Lizzie laughs and hits my thigh at his response.

"I know, but I want it to be special." She fidgets a little, obviously giddy. I stare at my best friend in wonder.

"You're in love?"

She bites her lower lip and blushes before she gives me a small nod. My heart swells with happiness as I take her hand in mine and squeeze. "With both of them?" I whisper, and I didn't realize how much I need the answer until I've spoken the question.

Biting down on her bottom lip, she meets my prying gaze and nods. "Both of them."

The relief is unexpected but so very welcomed. For the first time, it feels as if everything is going to be all right.

"So tonight they'll," I hesitate to say it but spit it out, "*both* claim you?"

Lizzie nods and for a flash of a second, I feel like she's holding something back.

"Do you have any questions about it?" Vince asks, distracting me from my thoughts.

"It happens under the full moon tonight, right?"

"At its peak," Vince adds with his nod.

"Not all of us at like once, right?"

"It's not an orgy. If you were hoping for that, you're going to be disappointed," Vince jokes and Lizzie laughs, sucking the last bit of her drink down and then shaking the cup to reach the whipped cream at the bottom. Vince's attention turns to Veronica, his voice softening. "We'll each go our own way, and enjoy our mates, biting down and claiming our love for them forever."

His gaze stays on her, but she fails to look back at him. Unease flows through me, but again Vince doesn't show concern.

"You two as well?" I question him.

He looks over his shoulder to nod again. "We'll run errands, get you two all settled and then," he says, peering back at Veronica and settles in his seat, "the night will come and the full moon will guide us."

CHAPTER 16

VERONICA

The branches crunch under my feet, the cool air gracing my shoulders. Peeking up through the canopy of leaves overhead, the full moon shines down, although the clouds cover it, providing little light to guide us.

My heart batters in my chest. He's so certain, determined. But since this morning, I've felt the advent of something else. It carries the air of betrayal and uncertainty. I haven't been able to shake it. It's a warning. I'm not sure who sent it or why, but as the hours ticked by, the feeling only strengthened.

"Who will be there?" I question as if nothing is wrong.

I am his mate and he is mine. Why does it feel as if destiny is warning me not to go through with this?

Squeezing my hand, Vince leads me through the forest so he can claim me. On the surface I do what I can to remain calm, but I'd be lying if I said I was unaffected. Fate has given my hard heart a mate. One mate to love with everything I have, and he's going to claim me as his. My nerves make my fingers tremble and I yank my hand from Vince's grasp before he has a chance to notice. Under a denser gathering of trees, it's dark and I can't see as well as he can, but I'll manage.

"Just us and the others with new mates. There's no need for anyone else to be there."

"So we'll all be witnesses to everyone else's claiming?" My pulse pounds, anxiousness climbing. I knew this would happen. I knew this was coming. I should have said something before now. A heat lingers on my skin, daring me to turn around.

Vince lets out a low laugh. "No, there's no need for witnesses. My bite will mark you and scent you as mine. You won't really be able to see anyone else anyway. This is the best spot for the moon, though. It's better for our wolves."

"I see." My mouth dries as we near an area with much more light than the surrounding forest. My heart races in my chest. One mate for all eternity. This is the beginning to a bittersweet end. I shake out my clammy hands and will away my tears. I'll outlive him by hundreds of years; I'll watch him grow old and die. And there's nothing I can do about it. The realization weighs heavy on my heart. But, as always, I shove my emotions into the depths of my cold heart and move forward. I've accepted my fate. It would be far too cruel to stop.

Even if destiny is warning me to do just that.

As we step into the clearing, the light from the moon provides a slightly better view, but it's still too dark to see more than a few feet in front of me. It takes a moment for my eyes to adjust, but I can hear what's going on with absolute certainty. Dom, Caleb and Lizzie are to the left, and Devin and Grace are to the right. No one seems to notice anything except their mates. Both women are obviously in heat, mewing and rubbing against their mates.

"What all does the claiming involve?" I quietly ask Vince as he unbuttons my blouse with deft fingers.

"We bond in the most intimate way possible and at our peaks, I scar you with my mark." His little fangs gleam in the moonlight as he leans down to nip my collarbone. It sends a shiver of want through my body. As my blouse falls to the cold, hard ground a chill hardens my nipples. His eyes focus on my breasts and he leans down to suck a nipple into his hot mouth. I moan and lean back, pushing my breast forward as the heat of arousal flows through me. A tingle of need flows through my blood. I'm obviously affected by the full moon, though not to the extent that the wolves and humans are.

As I open my eyes, they widen even further. I watch Grace on her hands and knees, pushing against Devin as he thrusts behind her, slamming his hips against hers. She meets every blow, moaning her pleasure into the ground. She arches her back as her body jolts over and over again. She whimpers as her body trembles, "I love you, Devin."

He presses his chest to her back and kisses frantically along her skin, never slowing his pace. "I love you too." His whispered words cause her body to shiver and convulse as he brings her to the edge of her release. He groans in satisfaction before biting into her neck.

My eyes shift to Caleb as he moves on top of Lizzie with Dom beneath her small body. "Please, please," she begs them, but I don't know what for.

"We've got you, little one," Dom murmurs in her ear.

"We'll take care of you, baby girl." Caleb slams into her welcoming heat. She screams out in pleasure as tears fall down her cheeks. Caleb kisses away the tears as he pumps into her, his hands roaming her lush body. Dom's hands squeeze her full breasts and strum along her clit as he moves in time with Caleb. Her head thrashes as the intense pleasure overwhelms her.

"I love you; I love you both so much." Her moan is nearly incomprehensible.

Caleb kisses her with undeniable hunger as they both pump faster into her. Her nails dig into his shoulders as they kiss, lick and nibble each side of her neck, preparing to mark and claim her.

My heart clenches as I watch them make love to her.

They may be beasts and they may be rough, but their love is unquestionable.

Vince's hand brushes along my back as he whispers into the shell of my ear, "It's time." His hot breath tickles my neck and I lean into his hard chest. Turning to face him, I trail my nails along his muscles. He rumbles a hum of encouragement.

I press my lips to him and push my breasts against his chest. "Take me, then." In an instant, Vince throws me to the ground, bracing my impact with his forearm. His ferocity takes me by surprise, but I allow his lips to crash against mine, and he kisses me passionately with frantic need. He growls into my mouth as he tears apart my skirt, baring me to him. My lips part to object and taunt his primitive behavior, but he shoves his hot tongue into my mouth, devouring mine with a fierce hunger.

Instantly, my worries are gone. I crave him. I ache for him. Is this the heat? Is this a part of being his? Succumbing to this desperation?

I've never felt a sensation so all-consuming. It's too much. Peering past him, the clouds clear from the moon, and the light brightens. Everything comes into focus with sharp clarity.

My breath quickens as he parts my legs and slams into me. I throw my head back in ecstasy as hot pleasure races through my body. He takes my exposed throat with his teeth, raking them along the tender flesh. My heart beats wildly, slamming against my chest as his pace picks up and my back scrapes across the ground with each forceful pump of his powerful hips. This is not my pup; this is my big bad wolf.

"Vince," I whisper as fear creeps in. It's a fear I haven't felt in a long time and for good reason. The beast of a man doesn't pause. It's as if he didn't hear me.

Vince's hand closes around my throat and pushes me down to the ground as his thick girth slams into me, stretching my tight walls, sending a pinch of pain through my body. I squirm in his grasp, but he doesn't relent.

My eyes widen as I comprehend, in this moment, that he owns my body. I'm completely at his mercy. Instinctively my hands fly to my throat and try to peel his fingers away. My sharp nails dig into his skin, scratching and scraping in a furious effort to pry my throat from his hold.

He roars as he continues to slam into me. Tears form as the memories flood me and I scream. The shrill cry brings a coldness that dampens everything else. His grip instantly lifts and I scramble to get away from him, stopping just feet from his hulking form. Landing hard on my forearms, I struggle to catch my breath. I close my eyes tight, willing the painful memories to go away.

This is Vince. My mate. This is Vince. My mate. I repeat the thoughts over and over, trying to calm myself.

When I finally turn around, my fingers brushing along my throat, I see Vincent's massive form on the brink of losing control. His silver eyes pierce mine with an intense, primal need and his fists clench tight. His shoulders and chest heave with every breath as a low growl rumbles through his chest. He's a beast in need. He needs me. I brace myself and swallow thickly. I can do this. I need to give him this. I get down onto my knees and face away from him before lowering my shoulders and head to the ground and parting my legs for him.

CHAPTER 17

VINCE

Veronica bows that beautiful body. She presents herself to me as a mate in complete submission, and my wolf howls in triumph. My tightly clenched fists push my body off the ground as I slowly stalk toward her.

Go easy, I warn myself. *Go easy on her.* I fight for control.

My hands stroke slowly down her back, causing her to shiver before gripping the flesh of her ass. I barely contain my need to pound into her. Moving my hips behind her, I lower my head to trail kisses down her shoulder. With my forehead resting on her back I choke out the words, "Tell me to claim you." Her thighs clench and the sweet smell of arousal overwhelms my senses as I groan in blissful agony.

"Claim me, Vince." At her words I pound into her welcoming heat to the hilt and still. Feeling her tight sheath pulse around me, I ride through her orgasm, pistoning ruthlessly into my fierce mate. She steadies herself as she whimpers, taking every forceful blow of my body. My fingers dig into the soft flesh of her hips as I pound into her, over and over. A cold sweat forms over my body. Her moans and trembling body have me growling and my spine tingling. But I'm not ready to come. I'm not ready to give this up. I flip her body over and immediately bite into the tender flesh of her breast, never letting up the brutal pace of our fucking. Taking her nipple into my mouth, I suck while my other hand digs harder into her hip as I slam into her welcoming pussy.

I savagely kiss up her throat and lick that delicate, pulsing spot in the crook of her neck. My claiming spot. Mine. My mate. Ecstasy is all I can feel.

My fingers find her swollen nub and I wait for her body to tremble and her pussy to throb with need. The tingling settles low in my spine and my limbs go numb as I near my climax. She shouts out my name with her release and I slam into her and still as I fill her with cum and clamp my teeth over her flesh. The tang of her blood fills my mouth, but I don't release. I feel myself pulse as her pussy milks every drop of cum from me. Cum drips down her thigh and onto mine. My wolf howls in victory of claiming our mate and it fills me with pride and a sense of completion. My heart settles with deep satisfaction. My mate, my other half—she's truly mine, now and for forever. After a moment to calm my breathing, I lift my heaving chest off of her small body and smile down at my mate. But the sight of her is nothing like I expect and concern quickly fills my now hollow chest. Her eyes are red with bloodied tears and her body is shaking.

"Baby?" I lean down to pick her up to soothe her panicked body, but she flinches and stumbles back, scrambling to put distance between us. My blood heats and my heart drops as I swallow thickly, trying to understand. Her chest rises and falls chaotically as her dark eyes penetrate mine with fear. "What's wrong, baby?"

She shakes her head, but doesn't break eye contact. "I'm not okay."

"Okay." Kneeling in front of her, I gently place a hand on her leg. She jolts from the contact, but I keep rubbing back and forth, letting our mating bond soothe her. After a moment, she calms and I scoot closer to her. "Can you tell me what's wrong?"

She swallows and her eyes dart left and right before she lowers her head. "Baby, just tell me." Tears threaten to prick my eyes like a bitch as I realize I was too rough with her. "Did I hurt you?" She adamantly shakes her head and my brow furrows. "I don't understand. Tell me what's wrong."

Her dark eyes finally find mine. "It reminded me." Her gaze drops to the ground again as shame washes over me. "It—

it reminded me." She doesn't have to finish. My hand falls as my world collapses, crumbling into an unrecognizable mess.

"It reminded you of—"

"Of why I started hunting wolves ... after what one did to me."

My breathing nearly stops as dizziness overtakes me. Our mating bond. Our claiming. The moment that was by far the most memorable experience of my life, reminded her of ... her assault?

"You were raped?" I don't know how I get the question out.

"Yes."

My hands on her body brought up traumatic memories of her past. Overwhelming nausea hits me, but I suppress it. Stumbling back, I fall on my ass. She moves to her hands and knees and crawls over to place a hand on my back, telling me, "It's okay."

"No. It's not." How could I let this happen?

I attempt to cradle her, but she recoils. Shame and guilt overwhelm me. With the pull of the moon, my mind whirls. Barely able to focus.

"What did I do specifically?" I question, and again attempt to comfort her, but she scoots back, avoiding my touch. "I will never do it again."

"I just can't. I can't be held down." It takes me a moment to feel grounded enough. Did I hold her down? When did I hold her down? I can't think, I can't control the shaking.

"How?"

"It's okay, Vince," she whispers, not answering my question. It's okay? None of this is okay. How could she say that?

My stern, hurt gaze finds hers as she tries to comfort me. *She's trying to comfort me?*

"Why didn't you tell me?" If only I'd known. I never would've held her down. I would've restrained myself.

"I thought you knew. That's why I need ... I have to be in control and it's okay." Her voice is soft and full of agony.

What the fuck? "That's why?" A twisted sickness fills my chest. I thought it was a game. I thought she was just playing with me. I need to leave. I've failed my mate in so many ways. I need to think. I need to make this right.

"You should have told me that." Anger swirls in my mind. I could have ... if I had let the pull take over ... the things I could have done ... the damage that would have been done ...

As I stalk into the woods clenching my fists and breathing hard, I barely hear my mate's soft plea. "Don't leave me." The need to take her again vies for control. My wolf begs me to claim her again, to prove that she's mine. To care for and to love, to have in every way.

I can't control it. This need to take her again and the fear that comes with it that I'll hurt her again presses down heavily, making me hate myself all the more.

My mate felt pain by being mine. I did that to her.

Peeking up from where she sits, the red streaks on her face are evidence of that and I take another step backward.

"Vince, don't you dare leave me," she threatens and she doesn't know what it does to me. Every instinct in me wants to unleash the needs of the claiming. To pin her down and—

Fuck! I can't. I can't hurt her again.

I would rather die than hurt her again.

I snarl as the tearing and cracking overtakes my limbs, morphing my human form into the beast taking over. She thinks I'd leave her? Anger consumes me. She's everything to me. I would never leave her, never hurt her.

And yet I have. I just did. Because she withheld from me. Controlling me rather than confiding in me.

Her veiled threat echoes in my head. *Don't you dare leave me.* Never in my life have I felt so lost and conflicted. My mind reels with the intensity of the moon seeping into my consciousness, wanting nothing more than to take Veronica.

I shake my head as my paws collide with the hard ground, hurling me forward through the brush. All I know is I need to be away from the moon, away from my mate, before I hurt her again. The cold air already has my lungs aching, struggling for breath. Good. I want to feel that pain. I push my limbs harder, wanting to feel the aching soreness throughout my body.

This isn't real. Denial seeps in. It can't be real. And yet, when she calls out again, commanding me to go back to her,

I know damn well it is real.

Commanding me. Because she doesn't know my wolf is threatening to take control. He doesn't think. He only acts. A menacing growl erupts from my chest.

At war with myself, I force myself farther away from her. Only to protect her, and yet she cries out that I'm her mate and I can't leave her.

How could she think I'd leave her? It's because she thinks she controls me. That if she falters, I'd run. I push faster on the ground. Barreling between trees and ducking under fallen limbs.

She needs to learn. She needs to learn to trust me like I trust her. I thought she did.

The moon threatens to wane as I approach the edge of the forest, breathing heavily and far too aware that the claiming is broken. I did not lick the wound clean. I did not lie with her after the deed, under the light of night.

How could I? With her in pain and our trust broken, that wasn't ever an option.

I will heal her. I will take away her control and give her true security. I will teach her to trust me. I've failed her as a mate until this point. I've let her hide her pain under the guise of control. No more. My silver eyes narrow as I sprint back to her. I'll take her away from the moon, away from any danger and I'll fix this. I'll make it right.

Veronica, my mate, I promise I'll make it right.

My conviction is firm: I won't rest until I've truly claimed my mate. Every bit of her. Her past and her future.

Only when I get there ... she's already gone.

This world has only just begun to unveil its stories.
Fate has been set in motion.

Primal Lust

Book 3 of the To Be Claimed Saga, is up next.

ABOUT THE AUTHOR

Thank you so much for reading my romances. I'm just a
stay at home Mom and an avid reader turned Author and I
couldn't be happier.

I hope you love my books as much as I do!

More by Willow Winters
www.willowwinterswrites.com/books

Made in the USA
Middletown, DE
28 October 2023

41487306R10102